DUST, DANCING

Other Books by Ian Gouge

Novels and Novellas

The Red Tie — Coverstory books, 2024
17 Alma Road — Coverstory books, 2024
Tilt — Coverstory books, 2023
Once Significant Others — Coverstory books, 2023
On Parliament Hill — Coverstory books, 2021
A Pattern of Sorts — Coverstory books, 2020
The Opposite of Remembering — Coverstory books, 2020
At Maunston Quay — Coverstory books, 2019
An Infinity of Mirrors — Coverstory books, 2018 (2nd ed.)
The Big Frog Theory — Coverstory books, 2018 (2nd ed.)
Losing Moby Dick and Other Stories — Coverstory books, 2017

Short Stories

An Irregular Piece of Sky — Coverstory books, 2023
Degrees of Separation — Coverstory books, 2018
Secrets & Wisdom — Paperback, 2017

Poetry

Bound — Coverstory books, 2024
Grimsby Docks — Coverstory books, 2024
Crash — Coverstory books, 2023
not the Sonnets — Coverstory books, 2023
Selected Poems: 1976-2022 — Coverstory books, 2022
The Homelessness of a Child — Coverstory books, 2021
The Myths of Native Trees — Coverstory books, 2020
First-time Visions of Earth from Space — Coverstory books, 2019
After the Rehearsals — Coverstory books, 2018
Punctuations from History — Coverstory books, 2018
Human Archaeology — Paperback, 2017
Collected Poems (1979-2016) — KDP, 2017

Non-Fiction

Shrapnel from a Writing Life — Coverstory books, 2022

Ian Gouge

Dust, dancing

First published in paperback format by
Coverstory books, 2024

ISBN 978-1-0686701-0-7 (Paperback)
ISBN 978-1-0686701-1-4 (eBook)

www.iangouge.substack.com

www.iangouge.com

www.coverstorybooks.com

Contents

✻

Playing Footsie with Burt Lancaster

Whether or not a consequence of the first time she saw him in *The Swimmer* Caroline couldn't be sure, but there was something about Burt Lancaster which floored her. At fifty-five he may have been slightly on the wrong side of his prime by then, but his masculinity, the way he prowled moodily, his physique, his voice, she found captivating. It had been enough — this relatively late introduction — to see her plunging into his back catalogue: *Run Silent, Run Deep*; *Trapeze*; *The Birdman of Alcatraz*; *The Train*; even *Local Hero*. Inevitably her favourite was *From Here to Eternity* and, on those increasingly rare occasions when Ron was humping away unoriginally on top of her, she imagined herself to be Deborah Kerr — just to get through it. More often than she'd like to admit, once Ron had exhausted himself she would retreat to the bathroom and, with Burt's help, 'finish herself off'. Her husband was inevitably fast asleep when she returned to the bedroom.

Fantasy being what it is, the fact that her idol was twenty years older than her proved no obstacle to passion; neither did the fact that in 1985 he lived on the West Coast of America and she in East Cheam. Occasionally on Sunday mornings when Ron was at church, Caroline would take herself off for a stroll around Nonsuch Park and imagine it a film-set for one of Burt's movies, propelling them both into a parallel universe where he and she could be approximately the same age and occupy the same small segment of the planet. Of course the film concerned would need to be an adventure movie of some sort, a vehicle for Burt to show off his athleticism, his heroism. Inevitably he would come and rescue her from the villain cowering in Nonsuch Palace. And once or twice, when sitting on a bench and looking towards the trees and bushes at the edge of the park, she would again imagine herself to be

Deborah Kerr, the sand and the beach replaced by a secluded carpet of soft autumn leaves. Whenever that happened, Caroline would shake herself mentally, force herself to stand, then begin the trudge home to prepare the vegetables for the Sunday roast. These were not appropriate thoughts for a woman of fifty-two she told herself, especially as the object of her affections was now into his seventies. Caroline knew that the underlying problem — and therefore indirectly responsible for these flights of fancy — was her husband.

There was an adage which suggested one should never marry the first person with whom you sleep; something to do with not being able to tell the difference between love and sex first time around, not having had sufficient experience of the latter to offer up comparisons. Caroline had become aware of this folklore far too late; not only had she already married Ron, but they had produced, in relatively quick succession, Elizabeth, Anne, and Charles (among other things, Ron was a staunch Royalist). Not that Caroline would swap her children for the world, of course. They had grown up to be normal, decent human beings who were now well into the same cycle to which she and Ron had succumbed — except for Charles who seemed pathologically unable to make any meaningful decisions about his life. Charles' dilemmas were, in Caroline's mind, compounded by an unshakeable notion that as soon as Ron had fathered a son he lost interest in her as a woman and them as a family unit. Thus he went through the motions as he was duty bound to (evidenced in part by his now sporadic attempts at love-making), but it had been as if Charles' arrival had flicked a switch, permitted him to shift down a couple of gears, to start coasting toward retirement.

In her case, the children forced a completely opposite response, and for the twenty five years between Lizzie's arrival and Charles's departure for university in Newcastle,

Caroline had to be at the top of her game — and the bottom of the priority list. She felt she had become invisible, unimportant; the role she performed and the functions for which she was responsible were vitally important to them all of course, but beyond their execution she became irrelevant as an individual with their own thoughts and feelings. Looking back, Caroline regarded the prime of her life as a wasteland. Yes, there were high points, moments of sheer joy, pride, affection, and as a unit they functioned well, were moderately successful; but as an individual she had shrivelled up, her essence hidden away inside the shell of her physical being. Perhaps that was why Ron was no longer stimulating for her: he had no way of recognising the woman he'd lost never mind finding a way to reach her contemporary self.

It was into this void that Burt had unwittingly swum. Flitting through television channels one wet Wednesday afternoon she had come across the film (already half-an-hour in) and been transported. Whether she had done so consciously or not, comparisons between her husband and this screen god were both inevitable and more or less instantaneous. And it had been an unfair fight. Ron had been crushed.

If she had been younger she might have done something about it. Going to California to seek Burt out would have been both impossible and preposterous, but leaving Cheam for a new life in England would not. Yet where would she go? What options did she have? She knew abandoning her present security on the basis of falling for an ageing movie star would have been insane, and if there was one thing she wasn't it was crazy. Hadn't she always been the one to navigate them through the tougher times — Lizzie being jilted, Anne's accident and the emergency surgery which saved her life — and the one whose role was to be the lighthouse charged with keeping their collective ship from the rocks? But now they needed her less, were away building their own lives and giving up on the one they already had. Who was to protect *her* from being dashed against those self same rocks? She knew the answer of course — it could only be Burt — but not only was he thousands of miles away, he had no knowledge of her existence.

When the BFI ran a Burt Lancaster tribute weekend she had no option but to go. Ron couldn't see the point: all the films would be on television at some point, or would be available on Amazon or iPlayer, so why waste the money? She gave up on her explanation half-way through its second sentence and went to get changed before leaving the house in good time for the nine-twenty-five train. As she sat watching the London suburbs slide by she realised that this trip to the South Bank was as close to adventure as she was ever likely to get, and for a few precious minutes was transported into a younger version of herself.

Although there were disappointingly few patrons for the first film, *The Crimson Pirate*, after a brief interlude for lunch numbers swelled for the second, *Sweet Smell of Success*. Secure inside her own little cocoon, for the best part of four hours Caroline was transported out of her humdrum existence and into different worlds, realms of adventure and drama and intrigue. It didn't matter that *The Crimson Pirate*'s music was cheesy, the plot a little thin, the Technicolour too vibrant; this was the world Burt inhabited and so it was just fine.

There was another break after *Sweet Smell of Success* during which Caroline decided she would go and sit in the café for a short while to recharge her batteries. And to decide whether she was going to call it a day or take in *Ulzana's Raid*. She had never liked westerns primarily because they were Ron's favourite and, having consciously rebelled against them for so many years, even one with her hero in might be something of a challenge. As she sat at a small table in the corner of the café staring at her tea and wrestling with her dilemma, she sensed a presence arriving in front of her and then someone sitting opposite her. The BFI was busy, but surely there were vacant tables — and anyway, wasn't it polite for people to ask before they gatecrashed? She glanced up ready to try some kind of polite admonishment.

Burt Lancaster, now sitting across from her, flashed that wonderful smile of his.

Caroline blushed instantly. Then realising how ridiculous the situation was, glanced away and then back as if to reset her vision. The man was still there. If he was a doppelgänger then the likeness was astonishing. Then he spoke.

"Which did you prefer?" That voice. This version of Burt — no more than five years older than she — was no cheap duplicate. "*Pirate* or *Success*?"

She swallowed hard.

"*The Crimson Pirate* I think." The words fell out of her mouth in what she was sure was an uncoordinated jumble.

He laughed. It was the same rich sound she had come to adore.

"People often do. But I suppose that's understandable in a way; adventure, excitement."

"Men in tights," she said before she could stop herself, instantly mortified at having made such a stupid remark to the person now sitting across from her — whoever he was.

It was enough to make him laugh again.

"And *Success*… I always wondered whether people liked my films with Tony because of him rather than because of me."

"*Trapeze*," she said. It was demonstration of a kind, proving her knowledge. And then: "But how can you even think that?"

"Because it's true? Because he was twelve years younger than me? And better looking."

She smiled, somehow in spite of herself.

"It doesn't become you to fish for compliments."

He leant forward just a little.

"That's better," he said.

"What is?"

"To see you smile again."

Caroline flushed once more.

"You were smiling through most of the *Pirate*, were you aware of that?"

"How do you know? Where were you? Were you watching?"

"I'm always watching," he said, placing his hands on the table.

Caroline stared at them. Were these the hands that had grabbed Tony Curtis's wrists when he attempted that death-defying somersault? The fingers that pulled the triggers on rifles and Colt revolvers to dispose of the bad guys? The same hands that held Deborah Kerr on the beach, the waves lapping around them?

"Penny for your thoughts. Isn't that what you say?"

She nodded. "Though probably worth much more than that."

"Let me guess." He allowed a pause to come between them. "*From Here to Eternity*, right?"

"How did you know?"

"I was lucky."

"Lucky?"

"To be playing alongside some wonderful people at the top of their game: Deborah, poor Montgomery Clift, Frank. People tend to forget that Sinatra was in it."

"And Ernest Borgnine," she felt the need to demonstrate the extent of her fan worship. "Donna Reed. She was so good in *It's a Wonderful Life*."

He was suddenly serious. "I would have loved to have been in something like that, but I guess it didn't fit who the studios wanted me to be. Or the movie-goers come to that."

"Perhaps, but you can't imagine James Stewart swinging on a trapeze can you?"

It was a comment which made him smile.

"Fair point." Another pause. "And anyway, it is you know."

Caroline was confused. "What is what?"

"It *is* a wonderful life. If Jimmy's film taught us anything at all it was surely that; no matter how low we get, there are always things to cling on to, that make life worthwhile."

"Like your movies," she said.

He eased back in his chair. As he stretched his legs beneath the table she felt one of them brush against her own. She left hers where it was.

"Like Lizzie and Annie and Charlie," he said, "though I know no-one calls him Charlie, but I'm American so you'll have to indulge me. And by the way, he needs your help perhaps more than you realise. I think there's a great kid right there struggling to get out from under; he just needs a little nudge."

She frowned momentarily, bemused as to his depth of knowledge about her family. Yet as soon as it had appeared the frown was gone, melted away by his steely yet benevolent gaze.

"And how am I supposed to do that?"

"Oh I think you know." He smiled again. "You just haven't quite worked it out yet. And anyhow, I'm hardly qualified to give credible parenting advice, after all I had three goes at marriage."

"And five children."

"Maybe so, but three goes at marriage… Whereas you've only needed one."

"To achieve what, exactly?" Although he had made it sound like a triumph, Caroline was instinctively unconvinced — largely because she didn't see it like that. Her tone betrayed as much.

"To have three great kids."

"And Ron? What about him?"

With his leaning forward again, she felt his leg move away, the gentle pressure on her calf suddenly gone. With a smile she found herself wondering if it would be possible to shower and not get that leg wet.

"Also only needed one marriage; and those great kids are his too."

Caroline looked down at her cup, then lifted it to drink what remained in it.

"I know, but…"

"You should get yourself another tea," he said, nodding to the cup as she replaced it on the table, "but before you do, can I make a suggestion."

"Of course. Right now you could tell me to go and jump in the river and I'd probably do it."

This time the laugh reminded her of Captain Vallo from the *Pirate*; it was full and rounded, and bore more than a trace of devilment in it.

"Nothing so radical. Or so wet. And don't make a joke about *The Swimmer*, I've probably heard them all."

She inclined her head, signifying acquiescence. Then, as she made to stand up, he put his hand on her arm to halt her movement.

"Ron needs your help too. Oh I know how you feel about him, that he's past salvation, that he's not the man he was etcetera etcetera. But that may not be entirely true. We're all fallible." He raised a hand before she could interject. "All of us, no matter who we are. I've been hauled up by my bootstraps more times that I care to recall — and always by a woman. Always. Some of us are luckier than others; and some — like the aforementioned Mr Clift — fatally unlucky. Not even Liz Taylor could save him, and she could have raised Lazarus."

He laughed to himself as if he had just shared a private joke with himself. Caroline recalled *Victory at Entebbe* and wondered if there was ever a spark between he and Taylor.

"All I'm saying is, don't give up on all this just yet. Over thirty years is a hell of an investment to throw away."

"That's easy for you to say," she observed. "You don't know Ron like I do."

He nodded. "That's fair, of course. But even so... Now, go and get that second cup of tea, and don't worry about *Ulzana's Raid*; it's not really your thing, is it?"

As she straightened, he let his hand fall to the table, and Caroline realised he had been holding her arm all this time.

"That's going to make showering really difficult," she said with a smile.

"I don't get you."

"More's the pity."

And then she walked away from the table and headed to the counter. Once in the queue, she looked back. He was still sitting at her table, staring intently at the space she had so recently occupied. How was that even possible?

A prompt from the barista pulled her from her reverie. She placed her order and watched them throw a tea bag into a mug, pour hot water on it, then listened to them bestow the usual instruction as to where to find milk and sugar. Jostled slightly between the counter and the bench where these were kept, a small amount of tea spilled from her cup. It was the kind of incident which would normally infuriate her — but not today.

Having added a splash of milk and a half-spoon of sugar to her tea, she turned and began to walk back to her table. Her coat was still on the back of her seat, but the other chair was now empty. As she knew it would be. How could it not?

Once back at the table, Caroline chose to sit on the chair in which Burt had sat, a choice which was going to make taking a shower an impossibility.

Closing his account

"There's not much room left."

"I don't need much more room," he says, looking at the tattooist in the mirror, the other man's head reappearing for a moment over his left shoulder. DK knows Ray has been staring at the last unadorned patch on his back and wondering if a regular income stream is about to dry up. Perhaps he is hoping he'll be given the office to start elsewhere. But DK knows there will be nothing more to be etched after today.

Ray gets back to work.

DK doesn't flinch like he used to. He tells himself this is because he has become used to the process, the pain; or that they have reached a part of his skin where there are fewer nerve endings. Largely, though, his increased tolerance is all down to Ray's skill. Ray had talked a lot about nerve endings in the beginning; it had a been patter akin to a Government Health Warning. But after his sixth visit the pro-forma changed as did Ray's attitude towards him. He'd seen people come into his shop with grand ideas about what they were going to have done, only to bail out far too early. "Fear," Ray said once, "or the pain. Or pressure from outside. All can culminate in the lack of bottle to go through with it." It was clear that he'd come to respect DK for his single-mindedness, for seeing it through — even though he had no idea what 'it' was. One visit each year, and for the last twenty-five years.

"When I'm done," the buzz of his gun stopping for a moment, Ray's head appears again, "are you finally going to tell me what it is I'm doing, because even after all this time I've still not worked it out."

DK laughs. Ray's plea has been a constant over the last few years.

"What does it look like?" DK had replied more than once. It was his standard comeback.

"A whole mess of things. Symbols and letters; words in some language I don't understand; little pictures a bit like those emoji things…"

There were indeed multiple languages, some modern, a few not; some of the symbols were hieroglyphs, some of the text was in Latin. Where DK had permitted the words to make sense and allowed English to stray into the image, they mainly comprised of quotations from writers, philosophers, poets — though to ensure incoherence they were never placed together and in the right order. That would have made things too easy, and puzzles should never be easy.

"It's story," DK always said, "a narrative."

"Well damned if I understand it," Ray complained.

"But if I told you what it said…"

"I know, you'd have to kill me."

They laughed at their private little Vaudeville routine — except Ray didn't realise that DK wasn't joking.

§

When did he get the idea? He tells himself it was when he'd had the 'accident' with Shona's yappy little dog, but suspects the seeds were sown much earlier than that. As a child he'd had what his mother liked to call 'little mishaps'. Some — like wetting the bed or tipping out the contents of cereal packets onto the kitchen floor — were nothing out of the ordinary. What little boy of four or five didn't do something to earn his parents' wrath? In DK's case, the 'parent' was singular, his father having abandoned his mother as soon as he found out she was pregnant. "It happens" his still-unattached mother told him many years later.

Whenever he'd done something wrong — especially if that wrong-doing resulted in her needing to spend money she didn't have — she'd tell him that she would add what he'd cost her to 'his account'; that one day he'd have to make good on what he owed. It was meant to make him feel remorseful. If there was a beginning, perhaps that was it: the notion that it was perfectly reasonable to keep a log of your transgressions in order to be able to settle them later. Gradually he began to have 'deliberate accidents' in order to see what she would add to his account. The knocked-over mannequin in the department store: added. The kid pushed off the swings: added. Fusing the lights when he tried to mend a plug: forgiven. There was a pecking order driven by the degree of cost, embarrassment or inconvenience foist upon his mother — and by his underlying intention. Hence the forgiven fuse. One summer, as he neared his teenage years, he took it too far and she threatened to have him taken away as she couldn't cope with him any more. He relented, and she agreed to wipe the slate clean.

And now DK's back has become his adult slate and, after twenty-five years of etching, it is nearly full.

Shona had been his first proper girlfriend. They'd met at a work Christmas party and fallen foul of a combination of cheap champagne and mistletoe. DK knew that they weren't the first to do so, and wouldn't be the last. He'd lasted a few months before he began to tire of her; but as he grew weary, Shona became increasingly keen. She started talking about "the future", painting pictures of a life he didn't want but which he could see drawing inexorably closer. DK's problem was that he didn't know how to extricate himself from her clutches. Shona had a small white terrier called Poppy, and Poppy hated DK with a passion. DK wondered if the mutt could read his mind and knew he was wanting to make good his escape. The more desperate DK was to free himself, the yappier Poppy became. In any conflict between the two of them Shona always took Poppy's side, said the dog knew DK didn't love it. From his perspective, Poppy was unloveable.

Which was one of the reasons he ran it over; that and to definitively prove to himself that Shona loved the dog more than she loved him.

DK pleaded innocence; said it was an accident; that he hadn't seen Poppy on the driveway. Shona was inconsolable — but retained sufficient acuity to finish with him there and then. DK had rid himself of both her and the dog in one swift push of the accelerator. "You'll pay for this!" Shona shouted after him as he left. Was it then he had the idea to re-open his 'account'? For no good reason he could fathom, when he got home he made a note of the incident; just the date, and two phrases: "R.I.P. Poppy", "goodbye Shona".

Writing it down made him feel better, though it wasn't exactly absolution. If anything, doing so proved the opposite, ensuring he wouldn't forget. But either way it was liberating. Perhaps terminating Poppy and getting away with it unconsciously brought back memories of the department store dummy and the kid on the swing. Something in him clicked, linking malevolence with record-keeping — and the notion that the second might excuse the former. His 'account' became his conscience.

There wasn't much to speak of that first year. When he looked back on it, his 'transgressions' were few and far between; apart from just a portion of one page, the notebook remained empty. At that point the sensible thing to have done would have been to tear out the page and throw it away. To forget the notion entirely. Yet it was a concept seeded so deep within him that he found himself unable to let it go. Not only that, his freeing himself of both Shona and Poppy seemed too important to ignore. The episode was worthy of record — and worthy of 'an account' too.

As coincidence would have it he had been reading John Irving's *Until I Find You*, a novel about a boy searching for his absconded tattooist father. The collision of the book's narrative with his own history, allied with contemplation of the year that had just passed, coalesced into a single fresh idea: he decided to carry his new account wherever he went.

If he was going to do this, the practical composition of his life-log was critical. He could hardly get someone to tattoo "goodbye Shona" on his skin. Not only might they not want to do so, but what if he ended up doing something truly despicable? It would be akin to transporting a visible confession around with him; he could never take his shirt off in public, never sunbathe or swim — and DK loved to swim. So he came up with a schema that involved pictures as well as words, with a few of the words not in English; a jumble of pieces a little like that you found when you first opened a jigsaw puzzle. Although there wasn't much to record that year, DK settled on his back as the ideal location to keep his history — and in doing so committed himself to the project for the long haul. He choose to begin with some Latin, 'in principio erat verbum' — 'in the beginning is the word' — though only 'verbum' made it to the first entry. Ray added the last word, 'principio', twelve months ago.

So for twenty-five years, unbeknownst to him, Ray has been etching DK's life-story on his back; the incoherent catalogue of all his misdeeds. And — inevitably — for the last five of those years he has also been pointing out that the available space was nearly used up.

There are two questions which have been exercising DK over a similar period. The first is how he should close his account. And the second is whether or not, having set out on this path, the tattoo had taken over his life; not in the physical sense of course — after all it was just a patch of skin — but rather whether DK's desire to keep the image fed led him to do things he would not otherwise have done? Had the tattoo made him a 'bad person'? Nature or nurture, perhaps. This second, more philosophical question, no longer remains unanswered as he sits one final time and submits himself to Ray's artistry, the other man working off the detailed sketch DK has provided.

This final session has been no different to all the others: DK presents his design, takes Ray through it, Ray asks his questions — mainly about size, colour, or the spelling of words he doesn't understand — then gets to work. The difference today is that DK has reached the conclusion that the tattoo *has* steered his life; that he *has* deliberately done things — seemingly ever more radical — in order to build an adequate inventory such that every year's entry into his account is worthwhile. When DK joked that he'd have to kill Ray if he told him all the things the illustration meant, he'd been truthful. After all, Ray wouldn't be the first. Not that DK counts his mother in that. In her case he is convinced he was doing her a favour, saving her from a life of old-age misery and loneliness as she slid inexorably into dementia. Better to go out with some faculties still intact. He'd got the idea for digitalis after using rat poison to kill a neighbour's dog who wouldn't stop its incessant barking. And when, like Irving's character, he eventually tracked down his father... Well, there could be only one possible outcome.

Would he have done those things without having had the tattoo to fill? He doubts it. But he has embraced his destiny, etching into his account as one might once have put a notch into a tally stick. And now the stick is full.

There is, of course, only one way to close his account. He has already settled on the means. It will be painless enough he believes, and most importantly it will leave his skin untarnished, his account finally become his confession. He only wishes he could be around to watch as they try to unravel what it all means.

Knowledge & Dreams

"What are you going to try?"

"If you think I'm going to touch one of those things you're crazy!"

Mik laughs at my protest. "They're brilliant. And perfectly safe. Just like the ads say. You should know that. Who would ever have imagined you could put knowledge in a pill?"

We're standing outside a *Knowledge and Dreams* ™ shop. The window is filled with lists and images, colourful depictions of locations, people, events from history. The products themselves — small individual little capsules — are kept locked away. Mik goes back to scanning the window.

"When did you first try one?" I ask.

"Me? I don't know. Two or three years ago? They were still relatively new then." He turns towards me, a broad smile on his face, a glint in his eye. "There was this girl I fancied. She was studying French poetry. I bought an hour of Baudelaire and had her in bed inside twenty minutes!" His sense of triumph is impossible to disguise.

"But that's cheating."

"She didn't seem to mind!" He laughs. "Though you're right of course, in one sense it was cheating — and which is why they've had to stop testing people using exams: pop a pill just before you go in and bingo! You know everything there is to know about Napoleon, or Shakespeare, or algebra."

"And afterwards?"

"Afterwards what?"

"With the girl; when your knowledge of Baudelaire disappeared after sixty minutes or so. Or had you won her over with your charm and 'prowess' by then?"

"Sadly only temporarily." Mik allows the smile to fade. "Turned out she was *really* interested in French poetry and not even my irresistible personality could compensate for an absence of credibility on the subject."

"And do you remember any of it — the Baudelaire, I mean? Would you recognise it now, for example? Or what if I asked you to quote me something?"

"You'd be wasting your time."

There are stories of exceptional people who'd managed to retain almost all the knowledge fed into their brains via those little capsules, rumours *Ke&D* ™ never chose to deny. When someone appears on television announcing that they'd kept the knowledge they'd paid for and were happy to be put to the test, there's no way to know whether they've simply taken another pill or had learned the subject the good old-fashioned way. What *Ke&D* ™ *do* choose to deny are the rumours that when the effects of their capsules wear off, not only do some people lose the temporary knowledge they've artificially acquired, but also something unrelated besides: the man who not only lost his brief knowledge of the 100 Years' War, but now no longer knew how to make coffee; the woman who, after a three-star *Ke&D* ™ experience, forgot her address and the name of her first child.

The total numbers of such stories — both positive and negative — are nothing more than speculation. From what I can see, Mik seems okay. Of course I have no idea how many times he has indulged; perhaps it depends on the number of women he wanted to bed! But he appears unchanged from the friend who'd initially experimented with Baudelaire; he's as cavalier today as he had been then. And he certainly hasn't been put off.

I follow him into the shop. It's all neon and glitz. *Ke3D* ™ have made extensive use of Artificial Intelligence in their image designs, their marketing; and even though the product is sold as 'high-end', the place feels more like a vape store or tanning salon. Undoubtedly having something in mind, Mik makes his way straight to the counter where a youngish woman in a white lab coat smiles her company-mandated greeting. I wonder how much of *her* is AI-generated or 3D-printed. I leave him to it, and turn to browse one of the touch-screen catalogues.

It's like an old Amazon interface: first you select a broad category, then narrow it down from there. Thinking about Mik's original experience, I choose literature and hone in on the old classics, the stuff no-one but University professors and students read any more. There are four levels of knowledge from 'one-star' through to 'four-star', and each entry in the catalogue is specific in terms of how long the knowledge will stay with you and how much you need to pay for the privilege. Charles Dickens is really cheap: 'one star' lasts six hours and costs just \$2; with 'four stars' what you learn hangs around for a week and sets you back \$12. Shakespeare is more expensive than Dickens, and the knowledge doesn't last as long; Orwell pricier again. It all depends how long you want to impress someone, and who that someone is. People assume that you get to know more 'stuff' the more you pay, that more stars represent a greater depth of knowledge in addition to the length of time you get to keep it; but *Ke3D* ™ are careful not to be explicit about that too — and how could you possibly know in any case? Yes, you could try all four experiences for a single subject in order to compare them, but if you'd already forgotten everything you'd learned between pills… Well.

I filter down to history and politics, which is where things get expensive! The closer the knowledge is to contemporary events, the more you have to pay; and if there is anything controversial about it…wow! Here the whole premise becomes something else — something darker some would argue — and where *Ke&D* ™ make the big bucks. The wealthier you are, the more you can know; the more you know, the more powerful you can become; the more powerful you are, the wealthier you get. There are groups of activists who occasionally protest against *Ke&D* ™, who say that the company is responsible for a growing divide between rich and poor, north and south, west and east. Sometimes their protests are large scale: the torching of *Ke&D's* ™ flagship Manchester store; attempted raids on production facilities in California, Russia, even China. They say *Ke&D* ™ is now bigger than McDonald's had ever been, that *Ke&D* ™ rules the world. Who could deny that with any certainty?

If, in order to keep up with things — especially adversaries and colleagues — politicians are popping handfuls of *Ke&D* ™ capsules before every session of parliament (and in every government around the world) who can possibly know what they are being fed in terms of content, facts, historical accuracy, truth? Even beliefs.

Mik appears at my side clutching a small recyclable glass phial containing a single bright yellow plastic pill.

"What did you get?" I ask automatically.

"That would be telling!"

"Something of interest to the young lady behind the counter?"

He laughs at my innuendo and glances her way. "Hardly. Once bitten, twice shy," and allows his comment to settle between us for a moment. "What are you going for?"

"Me?" I have flicked to the sports history pages. "Absolutely nothing. Some of this stuff is really expensive."

"Of course it is. 'Knowledge is power' and all that."

§

"What's the overall coverage?"

"Voluntary?"

"Is there any other kind?"

Both men laugh. Neither can see the other's eyes behind their thick sunglasses — which means they cannot know if the laugh is genuine.

The first man rises from behind his large desk and walks toward the window. The blind is closed which doesn't help ameliorate the gloom inside the room. He parts two of the slats and looks down onto the courtyard below; raining again, the sunglasses would hardly be any more appropriate outside. It has been proven that excessive exposure to *K&D's* ™ product can cause the whites of the eyes to take on what is referred to in headquarters as 'the twinkle'. Hence the glasses; no-one wants others to know how strong — or weak — their habit might be. Yes, 'the tell' is difficult to spot, but if you knew what you were looking for…

Company policy for internal meetings, Ryan is seeing more people in the public eye now wearing sunglasses: businesspeople, sports stars, politicians. *K&D* ™ has been selling their own brand of eye-wear in the stores for some time now; they are both functional fashion statement and profitable sideline.

"Around forty-six percent," Dalgliesh replies from where he sits.

"And the target threshold is?" Ryan turns back into the room, his hands fingering his glasses. His eyes have not 'twinkled' yet — nor are they likely to. He has been very careful; there is the long-game to be played. And by just a few of them.

"Anything north of fifty percent — though they say up-take has pretty much flattened out. There's a much higher customer base the further up the food chain you travel; not surprising really, given that's where the disposable income is."

"Indeed." Ryan resumes his seat, checks some papers on the desk. "And the micro-capsules?"

"Ready to go."

"At all four production facilities, and with a uniform profile?"

"Absolutely." Thanks to the sunglasses, Dalgliesh misses Ryan's slightly raised eyebrow; having an insight into what is *actually* going on in China and Russia, he is well aware that the truth may be slightly different. "We just need your 'green light'. Our new brand of *Your Best Life* ™ medicines — paracetamol, ibuprofen and aspirin — have been gaining significant market share since we launched them, and with our aggressive pricing policy we've undercut everyone in the market. They're being snapped up at the lower end of the economic spectrum. The business is happy to accept them as a loss-leader, as we planned."

"And what's the effect of inserting the micro-capsules into the medicines?"

Dalgliesh smiles. Ryan's convinced this one is genuine.

"Oh, people will still get a dose of their chosen pain-killer — though a slightly smaller dose admittedly. They'll also get a gift from *K&D* ™ which, for a short time, will make them want to visit one of our stores to indulge in the main event — almost irrespective of cost." Dalgliesh pauses. "The analysts are convinced that within a couple of months we'll see the headline numbers hit sixty percent. And then…"

Ryan waits for the word 'addiction', even though it is banned by *K&D* ™. But Dalgliesh is cleverer than that. It doesn't come. "And the FDA? People like that?"

"Let's just say that the people who make all the big decisions simply love our product — *and* the big discounts we've offered them."

If Dalgliesh is expecting a smile from Ryan, something reciprocal, then he is disappointed.

"Well then, let's get on with it."

§

"This place is a tip!"

I follow Lucy's voice to where she stands motionless in the centre of the kitchen.

"It's not that bad, Sis." Looking around, I'm sure I notice different things compared to those which leap out at her — and miss many of those she does see. She makes a move for the sink. "We do clean it up from time to time."

"Yes, when Mik's got some woman on the hook!" She dismisses my ineffectual protest. "You realise I'm only doing this because you're not feeling great. There are some ibuprofen in my bag. Help yourself."

"Thanks."

I plant myself in a chair and rummage through her handbag. My head has been raging on-and-off for two days now, the kind of sinus pain that goes with a heavy Spring cold. Having skived-off yesterday, work is something I don't have to worry about for at least a couple of days given it's the weekend, though I'm only too aware that there's a big project coming up for which I will be needed.

"Still bad?" Lucy asks.

"Dreadful."

"Man 'flu," she pronounces with little sympathy.

Once I've placed it on the table, the little medicine box seems almost radioactive, the clash between the brand's vivid yellows and greens almost violent. For a moment it appears something that shouldn't be touched rather than the budget medication it actually is.

"Are these any good?" I ask, lifting the box again and reading the unremarkable dosage instructions on its back.

"No idea," she says between the clattering of plates, "I've not tried them. Mum likes them, but I suppose that's because they're cheap. Can't see it makes much difference, one brand's much like another."

The unopened box is still on the table when Mik gets back from his run, Lucy recently departed.

"You've been busy," he says, admiring the tidiness. "I thought you weren't well?"

"Lucy."

"Ah, your guardian angel… You know, if she wasn't your sister…"

I laugh. "You'd still have no chance. She thinks you're a chauvinistic slob."

"To be fair, two of my finest characteristics."

As he takes his water bottle to the sink I get an inkling of what women see in him: tall, slim, undeniably athletic; charming when he wants to be, and a rogue when it suits him. That glint in his eye. The London marathon is just a month away.

"How far this morning?"

"Seventeen," he says in runner's shorthand. "Probably two more long ones and then I can start to taper. A couple of short runs the week before and then I'm off to the races! Three hours should be a breeze." He turns to face into the kitchen and sees the pill box on the table. "Head still bad?"

"Relentless."

"Are you going to take those?" He points to the ibuprofen.

"Why?"

"Don't you wonder why they're so much cheaper than all the proper brands? I mean, they may not have the same amount of oomph in them. They've cut costs somewhere — though clearly not with the ink on the packaging!" He walks over and picks up the box, examines it cursorily, then throws it back down. "Shower," he says; then, when he is out in the hall, "I don't suppose your gorgeous sister tackled the bathroom, did she?"

"She's not a martyr," I call after him. Mik laughs before he bounds up the stairs.

Two weeks later Ryan is sitting at his desk. His chair, reclined to its maximum, lends him the air of a man without a care in the world. Although the light on his speaker-phone glows green, it is silent, the sound being relayed to him through an ear-bud.

"As good as we expected? … Better? By how much? … And is that uniform across all territories, after all we expected the pick-up to be greater in places like the US. … Hmmm. And Russia and China? … They must be getting quite excited. … I think you know what I mean. … Indeed. And what about buying profiles? … 'Influenced'? How so? … Not exactly company policy — and not what they agreed to. But it's an indication, isn't? Exactly what we expected to happen; after all, the signs have been there for long enough. … Yes, as you say, 'old habits'. I assume they've also ramped up production? That would make sense considering what they're doing price-wise, and given the increased demand."

He allows the chair to ease him forward, then stands; begins to pace the room slowly.

"Are all controls and protocols in place? Or rather, I know they're in place, but are they being followed? … Well there's a surprise!" He permits himself a short pause. "Any sign of collusion? … No, between any of the parties concerned. I don't think we should rule out any geographic or political combination, do you? Stranger things have happened. … So it's essentially a race then? First past the post? … How long have we got? … You're sure? As little as that?"

Back at his desk, Ryan sits again, though this time upright in the chair.

"Everyone is ready, everything in place? ... Any doubts? Anyone you're concerned about? ... I know. But there are people like Dalgliesh everywhere. Can they get in the way? Yes, of course they can. But when they see which way the wind's blowing — or recognise the alternatives facing them. ... You're right, it may end up not being very pretty, but if it's coordinated to the minute and we act swiftly and decisively we'll mitigate collateral damage as best we can. ... I know, but what other choice do we have? What we've created, well, it's turned into something that was never our intention, obviously. And in the hands of monsters..." He laughs. "How could I not agree with you?" Another pause. "Why does it always come down to this? ... I hope you're right. ... Okay, so all we need to do is agree when. ... No, we'll tell the people who need to know — those who are going to do the dirty work — just thirty minutes beforehand. ... I know that's not much notice, but we have to mitigate the risks. ... And we'll be ready to take over the factories in terms of reestablishing protocols and controls? ... And the contents of the micro and critical capsules too? ... Yes, obviously. I assume the revised compositions are tested and ready to go, and that we can adjust the production facilities remotely? ... Thanks. I always had a hunch we might need a backdoor into the systems. Good job we've got some smart people working for us. ... When? Sunday week sound about right? Let's make it noon Greenwich. What time will that be elsewhere? ... Understood. But there is no perfect time, and we have to act everywhere at once; that's what matters most. ... Let's check-in same time next week. If anything comes up in the interim just let me know."

§

"Interesting look."

Mik removes his sunglasses to admire them. "Quite snazzy, I thought. Goes with the image."

"What image is that?" I ask as he replaces them on the bridge of his nose and his eyes disappear behind subtly mirrored lenses.

"You know: generally irresistible."

"Right — but only if irresistible now equates to sitting inside a dark and dingy pub on a Saturday lunchtime sipping orange juice and lemonade!"

"My body's a temple. At least until after the race next Sunday. Then I'll go to town."

"You won't be able to move!" As I scan the sparsely occupied bar I notice two other people also in sunglasses. "*Ke&D* ™ specials?" Aimed at Mik, I suspect I could just have easily posed the question to the other wearers.

"And why not? Good value — discounted when you purchase something else — and kind of cool-looking."

"And what was the 'something else' this time?"

"Actually, if you want to behave like my mum, a little package on the secrets of long-distance running."

"Very sensible."

"Glad to have your approval." He smiles. "And before you ask, I made notes, learned things that might be useful next week in terms of execution."

"Brains as well as brawn!"

Mik makes a faux bow. As he nods I can just see the tops of his eyes, the smile lines. "Very funny. But we both know you're the brains of the outfit. Actually, imagine if we could take your brains and my, well, everything else, we'd just about have the perfect man."

"I can think of a few people who'd instantly disagree with you."

"Like luscious Lucy?"

"Like Lucy indeed." I make a show of considering his notion. "But maybe you could sell the idea to *K&D* ™ — after all, they'll need another product once everyone's wearing their sunglasses."

§

She rings me two days later.

"How are you? The 'man 'flu' I mean."

"All good, Sis, thanks."

"Did you take those brufen? Did they help?"

I smile. Lucy often has a habit of running her questions together, creating a compound to which she expects a complete response — and which demands remembering all the questions.

"They didn't help because in the end I didn't take them."

"Oh?"

"I already had some stuff in the bathroom; you know, pills and potions."

"Those dreadful lemony drink things?"

"Yes, including those." I allow her space for a brief comeback. "But I was well enough to go to work on Monday, and now I'm fine."

"And how's Captain America? All ready for Sunday?"

I have a flashback to Mik sitting on the sofa the previous evening watching *Ninja Warrior*. "Far too relaxed about it. I'm sure he thinks it's going to be a breeze."

"Please tell me he's not wearing some kind of costume."

"Why?" I am suddenly concerned that I may have missed something between them.

"Because news travels. I don't want to become known as 'that woman whose brother lives with the twat who ran the marathon dressed as a cabbage'."

"And miss the chance of showing off his physique, his semi-sculpted six-pack, the thighs that could crush concrete?"

She laughs at the other end of the phone. "You have a point!"

I don't tell her that Mik has asked whether we are going to cheer him across the finish line as he smashes his three-hour target. Given I can't be there as I'm on emergency standby for work, I doubt she'd be interested in going alone. Either that or she'd be there to support someone else.

"What do you think about all this stuff that's going on?" Her voice takes on a sombre tone.

"Stuff?"

"The protests and speeches: Moscow, Beijing, Islamabad, Tehran, Washington. All of a sudden, out of nowhere. As if people have universally decided that they're unhappy and it's everyone else's fault. It's as if a fuse has been lit."

The tenor of the news has been increasingly downbeat during the previous week or so.

"Sabre rattling." I try to sound nonchalant. "The old prejudices resurfacing. Don't they always?"

"Here and there maybe, but everywhere?"

From nowhere I am reminded of the scene in the ancient and legendary *Ghostbusters* movie where all the ghosts escape at once: manhole covers pop as the spooks burst out; they fly out of drains and culverts, tube tunnels, waste pipes. I want to tell Lucy what we're seeing is a little like that — and remind her that in the end there are always Ghostbusters to save the day. But I don't. Partly because I know our reality is far more dangerous, and partly because I'm not convinced our modern-day Ghostbusters would have what it takes to save the world.

"They'll soon see sense," I offer. "Someone will make sure they see sense."

§

"What are we going to do?"

Dalgleish and Ryan are walking in the small courtyard garden at the back of the main building. It's the only place at work where Ryan can smoke. He knows it's a filthy habit and that he's one of the few left who do so, but at least it makes a small contribution to stress relief.

"Do?" Ryan echoes. "Why do you think we need to do anything?"

"I know you're up-to-speed with the news, the way things are escalating. I have it on good authority that our defence systems are on the verge of tipping over into 'amber'."

"Do you mean that stupid AI-driven software the government is now so reliant on?"

"Yes." Dalgliesh can't miss Ryan's contempt.

"Someone will see sense and switch it off."

Dalgliesh watches as Ryan flicks ash into a bin strategically placed for that purpose. He wonders if he is being tested.

"You think so? I'm not sure that's even possible." He doesn't wait for an answer. "But even if you're right, what about everyone else? The Chinese, the Russians?"

"Even the Americans?" Ryan smiles.

"And then there are the opportunists." Dalgliesh ignores Ryan's tease. "There will always be regimes who will try and take advantage."

Ryan cuts him a little slack. "You're right, of course. If things aren't perilous now, they may be soon. There seem to be far too few 'leaders' prepared to put their heads above the parapet."

"Perhaps because wherever you look the impetus is coming from the people, this sudden surge of nationalism. It must be difficult for them to go against that. Surely history tells us as much."

Taking a final drag on his cigarette, Ryan stops near the next bin. He nods at someone across the courtyard before disposing of the butt.

"That people get the leaders they deserve? Perhaps; though I'm inclined to believe it's more the other way round; that people tend to be vocal depending on what they've been encouraged to care about." He starts walking again. "How long do you think we've got?"

"Long?" Dalgliesh seeks clarification.

"Before some fool — or some automated system — presses a button they shouldn't? Or before they decide on invasion, 'boots on the ground'?"

"That I can't see," Dalgliesh says. "I mean, what would be the point? I'm sure some of our more muscular erstwhile friends would be happy to go straight to the end-game."

Ryan nods. "Same question though: how long?"

"From what I'm hearing — from friends in the government, the forces — the analysts are suggesting around a month."

"A month."

"Apparently there are a number of stages it's conventional we go through: claim and counter claim; accusations and denials. The first material threat, that's the real trigger."

Ryan lets a hand slip into a pocket and withdraw his cigarettes. The movement to take one from the packet and light it is practiced, automatic.

"So back to my first question. You're not suggesting that we should be the ones to move first, to make the first claim, first accusation, first threat?"

He has made sure the question is clear, heavy, loaded; it leaves Dalgliesh nowhere to hide should he answer in the affirmative. Ryan knows the Hawkish 'friends' to whom the younger man refers, just as he knows the esteem in which Dalgliesh is held. His is an opinion which seems to be carrying increasing weight, significance. There comes a point where such influence becomes dangerous, not only for Ryan, but for them all.

"I think we should consider it. Or at least be prepared to do so."

There it is, even with the not very subtle qualification. Ryan nods, feigns consideration. He looks at his watch, checks the date. Sunday is four days away. Time enough — just. But he determines to put his feelers out in any event, to check the temperature elsewhere, that *his* friends are holding their nerve.

He pulls on his cigarette.

"I think some kind of action may not be that far away," he says, maintaining his balance on the tightrope between truth and keeping Dalgliesh appeased — the same Dalgliesh who will inevitably be in the first wave of casualties.

§

Having finished his last prep run, I watch Mik as he packs his bag in readiness for Sunday morning. It is only Thursday. I have never seen Mik prepare for anything this far in advance, and I am struck by how relaxed he is, as if his tapering has been akin to the unwinding of a spring.

"Nervous?" I ask as we fumble around in the kitchen preparing our individual evening meals.

"About Sunday?"

"Yes."

"Why should I be? I've done all I can. The training has gone well; my last few runs have been good; there are no niggles or aches. Textbook stuff. And I know I can do the time. If we get away about 10:30 then I should be crossing Tower Bridge around noon, running down the Mall to the finish line ninety minutes later. Sure you're not coming to watch?"

"Work, like I said."

"And the gorgeous Lucy?"

"On her way to Paris as we speak — for a girls' weekend."

"If they were going to Amsterdam then I'd cancel the race and join them, if you get my drift… As it is, you'll both miss my triumph."

I laugh. "You're so confident."

"Only because I am." He cuts a few slices of apple. All bar one go onto his plate alongside a little cold pasta salad; he pops the last slice in his mouth. "I'm not trying to be cocky or bigheaded, it's just that I'm as prepared as I can be; I know everything I need to know, about me, my body, the course. And partly thanks to *Ke&D* ™, from my perspective it's risk-free."

On the other hand, for no concrete reason on which I can settle, I am feeling quite the opposite. If mine is a tapering of sorts too — work having gone very quiet — it is one which is so out of character, so unusual, that I can't help but feel it must portend something else, something unspoken. Unlike Mik, *my* spring is being invisibly wound. Without precedent, dates have been pushed back on the project on which I'm working (an upgrade to the finance system) and I've been asked to validate some old code, run a few tests, create a new subroutine to run against a copy instance of the database. In itself it's a program that seems to do nothing much at all — one parameter in, some data out — but I'm told there are 'other linked components' being developed and that I need to be on standby to run the subroutines on Sunday morning, possibly from the office. Weekend working is unusual, but not unheard of — especially in light of the way *Ke&D* ™ operates sometimes.

§

"Are any of our friends getting twitchy? ... Oh, that's concerning. Whereabouts? ... Saturday in London would be problematic; Berlin or Rome less so. ... Because it's the marathon on Sunday. If a bomb went off in the city on Saturday there would be a clamour to cancel the event. Which would only serve to agitate, heighten tensions. ... Exactly my point. Your information is credible? ... Indeed, though that's not a source we've needed to rely on for some time now is it? ... Have they given you any idea as to scale? ... Well, if it is more likely to be symbolic — execution of a small scale threat — that's the least worst scenario. Assuming it happens at all. ... Opportunists, as you say." Ryan hears the echo of Dalgliesh's voice in the word. The voice on the other end of the line continues speaking. "No, I think we hold our nerve. Only another forty hours or so. Given everything is lined up for then, if we tried to bring it forward — even by an hour — we run the risk of missing a vital piece of the jigsaw, and it's risky enough already. ... Of course. ... So the 'go / no go' call is booked for ten on Sunday? ... Good. And I agree; at this stage I too can only see one outcome. Let's hope I don't have cause to speak to you before then."

§

Standing in the kitchen waiting for the kettle to boil I realise I've left my phone in the car. Mik wanted a lift to the station having arranged to stay with a running friend near Greenwich overnight: "to eliminate the last variable from the equation". As I go out to the car I find myself wondering if I have ever seen him quite as prepared, organised.

It is only when I pour water onto my coffee that I pull out my phone to check it. A message from Lucy: *I'm fine. Don't worry.* Knowing she arrived in Paris the previous afternoon, I'm not sure what I'm supposed to worry about; lecherous Parisian men, perhaps.

An hour or so later, as I settle with my spartan lunch in front of the television, I realise the reason for her text. The news is filled with the bomb in Paris; six dead, twenty or so injured. Significant in size, it had been planted in a business district always quiet on Saturdays.

I phone her immediately.

"I said not to worry," she says immediately on hearing my voice. Then she laughs at my concern.

"You weren't anywhere near it?"

"Actually we were up the Eiffel Tower when it went off. It was truly bizarre. We happened to be looking that way when it exploded. There was this dull thud and then a pall of smoke emerged from between buildings somewhere. As you can imagine, there were shouts and screams and lots of chatter."

"But nowhere near you?"

"I said no. In fact our hotel is on the other side of the city, so we're fine. Really."

"And now?"

"What do you mean, 'now'?"

"The city."

"There are police everywhere." Lucy pauses momentarily. "And a lot of nervousness. You can feel it in the air. They think it might have been some militant group from the Middle East, which is making people edgy, given how cosmopolitan Paris is."

I sense hesitation. "And?"

Lucy lowers her voice. "Well, I'm here with Daisy and Shaz, and she very clearly fits the profile — if you see what I mean.

So we're back at the hotel, waiting for things to calm down. Apparently in some districts there's some unrest."

I overlay her words onto the images I see on the screen. There are groups of men wandering the streets. In any other context, given it's Saturday they could be football fans.

"Best stay there," I suggest.

"Don't worry; we'll look after ourselves. It'll be back to normal tomorrow and then we can go sightseeing again. How's the bionic man?"

§

"Our offices? … Well, if it was only a few windows — though that in itself seems like a warning, don't you think? If they'd wanted to, they could have caved the whole place in. … Indeed. No rumours of anything else, either in Europe of further afield? … Yes, I expect some people are a little bit nervous. Those itchy trigger fingers!" Ryan tries a small-scale laugh; it feels as forced as it is. "No, I expect that's it for today. There will be conversations happening all over: Governments trying to work out what it means, what they should do. If our plans work out, perspectives will have changed by this time next week. … Yes, good point; it *will* be interesting to see who moves in that direction first. It will tell us a lot about them as individuals of course, as will the reaction of their colleagues. Any thoughts about who that might be? … I can't disagree; the more addictive cultures, shall we say? Anyway, unless there's a sudden escalation, ten o'clock tomorrow."

§

Although I'm not entirely comfortable in the role of 'big brother', Lucy's text early Sunday morning puts my mind at rest sufficiently for me to settle down in front of the television to watch the start of the marathon. Not being there, this remote support for Mik seems the least I can do. I've no expectation of seeing him of course, but you never know; beyond the wacky costumes of the charity runners, his is the kind of physique a television director might choose to settle on for a couple of seconds.

Greenwich Park is rammed, a whole mass of humanity ready to embark upon a shared quest, all chasing the same dream.

Just after ten o'clock, with the elite men now on their way, my phone buzzes. I assume it's going to be a message from Lucy telling me that all is now quiet and the three of them are on their way to Napoleon's tomb or somewhere, but instead find something from my boss: I need to get to the office, retest my new subroutine, schedule it to run at twelve precisely.

§

The building is quiet. Few people work on a Sunday. When I arrive I find a second security guard at the entrance checking passes, and a third who escorts me up to the IT suite. Two other colleagues are already there.

"All a bit cloak-and-dagger," one of them says as soon as the guard has left me there.

"Let me guess," the other, directly to me, "you've written some kind of subroutine that doesn't make any sense in itself, but that needs to be run at twelve precisely."

I nod.

"Welcome to the whacky world of *K&D* ™!"

All three of us finish our testing — including cross-checking our work with each other — and have the programs set to run when requested. It's eleven forty-five, so we move to the rest area and turn on the television while we're waiting. Runners are pouring over Tower Bridge.

"I know someone running," I say. "He should be coming over the bridge soon."

"*Everyone* knows someone running," is the response.

I say nothing, suddenly absorbed by people dressed as fairies, wresters, characters from *Star Wars*, superheroes, all making their way over the river.

Tower Bridge is half-way.

§

Around the world clocks chime. In multiple *K&D* ™ offices, fragments of newly-written computer code start running; within minutes there are subtle and unseen changes in manufacturing facilities worldwide, compounds are slightly adjusted in all capsules, especially micro-capsules. Deliveries are halted mid-transit as production is briefly ramped up to cater for a temporary shortfall created from the unexplained disposal of millions of *Your Best Life* ™ tablets. Some offices are deadlocked remotely, and for some people access to buildings, systems, telephones are automatically removed. A number of these people, oblivious to what is going on, are roused by a knock at their door, taken by surprise at being suddenly overpowered, incarcerated — people like Dalgliesh.

In his office, Ryan begins to scan his message channels, makes a note of progress, ticks things off a mental list. Calls start coming through to him; brief calls containing code words, confirmations, the occasional question.

On Tower Bridge, Mik waves at a camera, the director lingers on him for a moment, this picture of health who's smiling, confident, bang on schedule. But I miss him, back at my desk, checking that my code has worked as expected. And I also miss Lucy's message which tells me she is in a queue to go for a ride on the Bateaux Mouches.

The coup — on the face of it not much more than the result of internal corporate in-fighting — is over in less than twenty minutes. I miss that too, as does just about everyone else on the planet. As the new week starts, sixty-plus percent of its population continue to pop *K&D* ™ capsules, and by the middle of the week there is a change of mood as politicians of all persuasions find themselves inclined to be more conciliatory, forgiving. New accords are tentatively struck; amber reverts to green. Those responsible for the bomb in Paris are quietly handed over to the authorities. It is talked of as a pivotal moment.

§

Sitting in his office high up in *K&D's* ™ corporate headquarters, Ryan knows different. More than anyone else, he has the whole truth.

"Ladies and gentlemen," he says, opening a conference call on Monday morning, "well done. I hope you realise what we have achieved. What *you* have achieved. We have helped people take a step back from the brink; we have reasserted all that is important, valuable, sacrosanct. We have used our modest influence in the best possible way — and we have done so invisibly, discretely. There will be some colleagues you will miss; not many, but if they are not there you will know why. And hopefully you will not be surprised. Indeed, you shouldn't be. But *you* are there, and that is testament to something special." He pauses to allow a spontaneous round of applause to run its course. "But we have only just begun.

Now we have proven what we can do, we know what must come next."

§

That same Monday morning I am back at my desk, unaware of the conference call. Just as I am unaware of Mik returning home proudly wearing his marathon medal, his reward for two hours fifty-eight minutes and seven seconds of running. I am unaware too of Lucy and her friends boarding their plane, in her luggage a cheesy souvenir replica of the Eiffel Tower and a t-shirt saying "I love Paris" which is to be a gift to me.

And I am unaware of what is to come next, and how the world is about to change forever.

Gone with the flow

I never meant to drop my shoes into the water. It was an accident, a momentary lapse. But if I hadn't done so, imagine that; everything which followed on would have been different, there would have been an alternative. Something other after the river — in gratefully accepting my fallen shoes — embraced them, conveyed them down to the weir where they tumbled over its edge like little boats. Unmanned boats. Or un-manned. If you had been standing on the shore, perhaps mid-way through a picnic, and looked up at just that moment and seen a pair of shoes, one after the other, tumbling onwards, what of them would you have been able to make out? Style? Colour? Certainly not left or right.

But then none of that actually happened, did it? Certainly not the river — at least not as we once understood rivers to be. Nor the picnic. When was the last time you'd had one of those? A decade ago perhaps.

I *did* accidentally knock my shoes from the bridge, that part's true. I shouldn't have taken them off of course, but it was so hot (as always) and I wanted to give my feet a chance to breathe, even if that's a ridiculous notion. So I looked down to where they had fallen — forlorn in the dry riverbed's dust — and allowed imagination to take over. That and a slice of memory. It was a cocktail, perhaps. I'm sure you remember cocktails!

And then there I was, scrambling down the bank, trying not to cut my feet on the exposed stone. Strange how it felt like a rescue. But these days (these years!) we'll take any opportunity to make such a claim, won't we?

You'll forgive my flight of fancy earlier; all that stuff about the picnic… I'm not as prone to them — flights of fancy, that is — as I used to be. Compared to before, obviously. But I'm exhausted thinking about how things are, as if I've had enough of the shock and horror. And the grief. Enough of trying to come to terms with how we got here, to a dust-dry riverbed — and of trying to forget how life had once been. For both of us, separately and together. Who hasn't been worn down by all of that? Anyway, I'm trying to ease myself back in. Not into how it was of course — that's impossible! — but to elements of my old life: remembering things, constructing scenarios. Even writing again. I suppose it's a kind of re-living, in a way embodied by that fantasy about the shoes on the bridge; the shoes I actually dropped.

And in processing what happened in my present reality, I couldn't help but think about what would have happened in the old one. You might choose to think of it as occupying a parallel universe if you wanted to, if that helps in some way. Remember when that particular theory was all the rage? But there I go again, imagining you, imagining things that can't possibly be; entertaining dialogues that are not of this or any other moment. It's as if I want there to be another 'now', and that putting words down is a means of creating an alternative which is tangible and better. Is that what writing does? The function of words? And when life *was* perfect — when the river flowed and we had picnics on verdant riverbanks such as the one I've fleetingly and only partially reimagined — what was the purpose of words then, given we already had it all? Even if we didn't know it… What had I been trying to achieve then in comparison to now, especially when this 'new' writing seems to offer the opportunity to be — I don't know…

Where does all that anchor me: back in an unwanted past, or in the indisputable present? And if the latter, is it the concrete, tangible and undeniably real present, or the one I wish could be real?

Sometimes I wonder about 'the future' too and what that looks like, and whether or not I should be casting my gaze toward a different horizon, consider what might happen if I were to drop my shoes from a bridge in *that* world. But when I do, I inevitably decide that dealing with one past and two versions of the present is more than enough for anyone.

Where have all the lapwings gone?

It seems like only yesterday. But then it always seems like only yesterday. I was walking here, along this very lane, the late Spring wind still harsh and unrelenting enough to demand a decent coat. And as I walked, I was accompanied by lapwings rising up from the fields on either side, keeping pace with their somehow haphazard flapping. It was as if they hadn't quite got the hang of flying. And their calls, piercing and insistent, were like those of less-than-secret agents passing on an urgent message they were determined to get through.

I may have talked to them. Huddled inside my warm coat, perhaps I felt some kind of acknowledgement was warranted considering they were the ones making all the effort. At least it seemed that way. And it would have been perfectly acceptable to do so; talk I mean. And by 'perfectly acceptable' what I'm really implying was that there would have been no-one else about, no-one to have heard me and assume I was a little soft in the head. Which meant no-one to interrogate me either. *What did you say?* they might have asked. Would that challenge have been worse than an assumption of madness? It seems odd to say so, but yes…

In any event, here I am again: the same path, the same time of year. But without the lapwings. I have even paused — more than once, just as I do again — in order to give them a chance to rise from their ground-nests, to swoop the rough hillside, to keep in-step; but there are none. Yes, there are occasional birds, little things that flit more than fly; birds who keep their distance, whose 'pip' is more a chirrup of annoyance than engagement. And I don't know their names. It is difficult to establish any kind of relationship under such circumstances.

All of which means that, without the lapwings, I have nothing immediate, alive, present, to converse with — which is where you came in, even though you are none of those things.

If I wanted to be obtuse, disingenuous, I might suggest that you had been here more often than me — if I wanted to stretch the point beyond breaking that is. But this is hardly your kind of landscape. Not that you didn't appreciate the countryside when seen through the windows of a coach or train. That was your limit though, engagement through a pane of glass at sixty miles an hour. Walking boots and a good waterproof never adorned your lobby never mind your person. I have never asked myself why that was until now — because of you easing your way into the void left by the lapwings, I suppose. I might have said 'elbowed' your way in, but that would hardly be fair, not your style; I left the door open, the invitation made some time ago. Not immediately upon your death, of course; then time was taken up with practicalities and the minutiae of embryonic grief. Nor later as I waited for something else to kick-in, emotions I assumed would assault me one day, knock me sideways. But they never did. And haven't today. Rather your presence has meandered its way into my walk, almost apologetically, announcing your proximity in that obsequious way you had, appearing to require approval to exist from anyone who happened to be remotely in your sphere. Well, you haven't needed to do that for a while either, have you?

How long has it been? I must have been wondering that too, I suppose. There will have been a trigger that brought you to the forefront of my mind, something that meant I was primed to replace the absent lapwings with images of you. It was the images that came first. Not you in a coach or a train, cooing out of the window at the passing greenness, but rather bent over a sink in that dreadful semi-nylon housecoat that seemed welded to you; or pushing our old antiquated vacuum cleaner over increasingly threadbare carpets. Nothing romantic. Not that you will be surprised by any of that; disappointed perhaps, but not surprised. My guess is that you would have preferred me to recall other moments, other sets of circumstance, ones that meant more to you than me — and therefore probably forgotten by yours truly along the way. A child's memory is very selective, don't you think? As we age and our lives gain a sharper focus, so the past inevitably blurs and with it history's inhabitants. More or less. There comes a point — if you subscribe to such a theory — beyond which memory starts to be about loss rather than acquisition, where the importance of the new, the present, consigns earlier days to some graveyard of the relegated. Gradually the once-connected become strangers. Absence doesn't make the heart grow fonder; that's poppycock. It makes it grow colder; after all, there is no attribute in distance allowing us to keep the flames fanned.

If I met a dog-walker right now — just as I did when I was last here, having turned at the end of my stroll and begun to make my way back to the warmth of a temporary abode — and they were to ask me about you, *Tell me about your mother*, what might I say? Platitudes probably, spouted largely because they were expected, true or not. *Describe her.* The housecoat and the hoovering would be a safe place to start, perhaps followed by an incident from a summer holiday, or the way you cried when your own mother died. Or would I stray into those half-imagined things seen by a child but not understood until much later when wisdom began to come knocking (though inevitably far too late). Was there anguish each time we were forced to move house, anguish disguised by a brave face and 'stiff upper-lip'? Frustration that your husband — my father — failed to live up to his side of the matrimonial bargain when it came to 'cherishing' and 'honouring'? Anger that he choose to leave you for good when succumbing to the heart attack that did for him on the way home from football one Wednesday evening. What does it say about me that I can still remember it was a cup game? Not only do I recall the score, but the scorers too: Hiron and Trebilcock. Yes, that doesn't say much. Or a great deal, depending on the lens you choose to view me through.

I suspect your lens was always the same, tinted with benevolence and believing in the best. Given I was your only offspring what choice did you have? You had no fallback position, no reserve, no-one up your sleeve. Though not for the want of trying? I wouldn't know — though I could guess. Perhaps rumours about the Old Man were swilling around even then, had reached your ears; and news or not, who could blame you for pulling up the drawbridge? I wonder if that's when you began to be alone; not strictly speaking of course (not for a few years anyway) but metaphorically, emotionally. There was always something I sensed you wanted from me that I was unable to provide. Or unwilling, consciously or otherwise. Perhaps that's part of the answer to the dog walker's question: *she always wanted something I couldn't give her*, I might have said. Vague but possibly enough to satisfy them for a few moments — until the follow-on question, anyway.

But what if I tried to get my question in about the lapwings first. *Where are they?* I'd ask. Then I'd describe how I'd been here before and been entranced by them — but not confessing to having spoken to them, of course! *Ah, the lapwings*, my temporary friend might say, falling into step; then they would scuttle off into a verbal cul-de-sac filled with their knowledge of natural history, the back-and-forth of the whole package sufficient to occupy us for many yards, close enough to the end of my walk not to leave too big a gap to be filled. A gap in time not space, you understand. But not only are there no lapwings there is no dog walker, just me and the wind, my good coat and heavy shoes. And now you, silently walking just behind me, a step in arrears, somehow servile. Was that how you saw yourself for all those years? Did you regard yourself as my servant — especially after the Old Man died? If back then *I* was the person who needed to be led, I suspect it was a requirement you never recognised. Maybe I didn't give you the chance to do so. Did there come a point when I saw myself as 'the man of the family'? The only male, certainly. If so, how misplaced was that — especially as I abandoned you at my first opportunity, choosing to abscond to a university so far away as to make any journey to see me an impossibility for you? Whether or not either of us realised it at the time, it was an exercise in control. Somerset to Edinburgh is more than arm's length, wouldn't you say?

Distance; maybe that's the one constant, the thing that categorises our relationship. Perhaps we were never close. It would explain a great deal, wouldn't it? How I remember things; how I behaved, perhaps; the decision to go and live in Scotland for so many years; my inability to cry at your funeral. Or subsequently. And even now, walking this cold road on the edge of the Pennines, you still in my wake, silently kowtowing, subservient, letting me call the shots. And saying nothing.

Ahead, the large house where I'm staying comes into view, thin spirals of smoke rising from one of the chimneys, the fire now lit in the front room. With the road beginning its slow downhill arc toward warmth, the wind gradually falls in behind me. I check the sky again, still hoping to see the lapwings. Maybe next year.

The Anthracite Crow

It's like being typecast — only worse. The assumptions people make, based on what? Colour primarily; that and a beak which looks as if it could do some real damage. And it could! But then again, isn't that what you'd expect from 'a scavenger', to find him armed with a weapon suitable for some nefarious activity like picking at, drilling into, tearing from?

Then there's that old joke about one of us standing a little way up the road on sentry duty, ready to call out "Car! Car!" to prevent our kin being run over.

I say 'kin' and not 'kith' quite deliberately. Because 'kith' would have to include cousins with theoretically redeeming features: the magpie, who actually shimmers dark blue and purple in a certain light; the hooded, whose black gives way to grey in the impersonation of a dapper butler; the large and censorious raven whose cachet comes courtesy of the Tower; or the jackdaw — somehow the jester of the party — forgiven his indiscretions because, well why wouldn't you?

Don't be fooled by the variation in garb, there's less difference between us than you think.

I should have been white; did you know that? In fact I was white an age ago. Resplendent, almost revered. Until the day I found myself the bringer of bad news. Wrong place, wrong time. It's something that's become a common rap. When we were white, no-one would have dared to think us gossipy or quarrelsome, or a betrayer of love or religion. But now we are defined by our blackness. Or have been redefined by it. The negative sticks to us as if our feathers had been turned to velcro in their darkening.

Think 'crow' and you think of 'black'. Think 'black'… Well, not much of what you'd come up with would be very good, would it? And even those who pretend to celebrate us do nothing to dispel our tabloid image. The night-time sea is "crowblack"; we are "head-down in the beach garbage", or we "stab and stab", "bent in emptiness". If only we *were* "stronger than death"…

People who come to this museum and peer into this glass prison (in the main, a certain non-black kind of individual) often do so with the words of poets resounding in their ears. Their eyes gloss over us as they scan the display for the brighter colours, the small and dainty, the unusual. Our characters have been pre-painted for them, and our blackness makes us almost invisible, unworthy. We are both ourselves and our shadows simultaneously. Perhaps that is all we are now, a shadow. Or that is what we were turned into by Apollo an eon ago.

If we had still been white today, what then? How could you not admire our glory, endow us with the positive? I might be able to declaim "I am a crow!" with pride, knowing I would be treated with reverence, rather than as the obvious guilty suspect in an avian identity parade.

Fault lines

"Tell me all your faults."

I laughed, assuming she was joking. And though there was a slight smile on her lips, her eyes betrayed earnestness.

"You're not kidding."

"Of course not. I'd like to know what I could be getting myself into. Potentially, I mean."

Nodding, I feigned understanding. Yet even that simple sentence — and it's qualification — provoked a myriad of further questions needing to be answered: mainly what did she have in mind? Then drilling down, did what she was thinking correspond to my own objectives, hopes, ambitions — or was she taking all that for granted, having read me well enough to decipher them? Perhaps I was that transparent. Perhaps she thought she might triumph where others had evidently failed.

"And how would you like to define 'faults'? A distaste for soft cheese, perhaps? Or an abhorrence of right-wing politics?"

She shrugged her shoulders. Although the smile seemed benevolent enough, I didn't yet know her well enough to be confident of that. My desire understand — to deconstruct her, if you like — was, from my perspective at least, at the core of our being together, sitting drinking beer outside a canal-side pub on an early June evening.

"Your choice, of course — though imagine how it might be received if you were to be too frivolous?"

"So if I told you that, as a young man, I once had a crush on Ann Widdecombe…?"

"I'd leave without finishing my drink." Her glass was two-thirds full.

"You're serious then?"

"Aren't you?"

For a moment a slight cloud seemed to pass across her face as if doubt had briefly cast its shadow there before being blown away. Just beyond the towpath a narrowboat made its way toward the flight of locks some half-a-mile distant. I allowed it to take my attention for a moment, an interval I intended to use to settle on a tactic.

Knowing I was compelled to answer her (I had conceded that much already!) my first few responses — and how she took them — would set the tone. I looked at my glass.

"I like beer, but not lager; wine but not spirits. My favourite crisps are cheese-and-onion or, sadly, Bovril when can I get hold of them. I like broccoli but not cauliflower, nor mange tout, runner beans or mashed potato."

She was smiling but shaking her head.

"How am I doing?" I asked.

"Shall I get my coat?"

"Not 'faulty' enough?"

"Not even close."

"Give me a clue."

"Okay." She paused for a moment. "I love my mother and despise my father — and at least one of those is a mistake."

"Heavy stuff." I'd already got the impression that she was a sincere person, but hadn't sounded the depth of her honesty. "Which one?"

The smile returned. "It's not my turn yet. And I asked first."

If I was to impress her, 'pass GO and collect £200', then it would take some effort on my part. For an instant I wondered whether I shouldn't be the one to stand up and walk away. But in that moment, and as that thought bounced across my synapses and off into the ether, I knew I couldn't because once again I was already trapped. This — she — wasn't going to be easy.

§

- I met her a couple of times. Or three, maybe. She'd put an ad in the *Gazette*; you know, one of those lonely hearts ads — though when I met her I couldn't understand how she could possibly be lonely. Know what I mean?

- Why did you think she couldn't possibly be lonely?

- Because she was so beautiful. Sculptural. That's what I ended up thinking. If she'd been made of marble, someone would have put her in a gallery or a museum.

- Untouchable?

- In the museum? Sure. Why would you let people put their grubby hands all over her? I mean.

- Where did you meet her?

- Once in a Costa — the one just off the High Street. That was the first time. We had coffee, talked. You know how these things go, sparring like a boxer: I tell her about about me, she tells me about her. Not all of it true, obviously. Back-and-forth, ducking-and-diving.

- You lied?

- Doesn't everyone?

- Did she like you?

- Of course. I mean, she agreed we could meet again didn't she? It's not like I forced her into anything. Is that what's you're implying?

- Where was that, the second time you met?

- In *The Lobster*. You know, that pub just up the hill from the park. Or part-way up the hill. That was my choice, not hers.

- Isn't *The Lobster* quite sophisticated?

- You mean expensive, don't you? But we didn't get anything to eat. It wasn't that time of day. Just a drink. I had a lager shandy, and I think she had a coke. Or an orange juice.

- Lager shandy?

- Well, I didn't want to risk anything. Not that I drink much any more; you understand that, right? Just occasionally now. And it was early, so we weren't eating. Like I said.

- What did you talk about?

- The same sort of stuff. Oh, and she asked me about holidays; you know, where I'd been, where I'd like to go. Turned out she'd been to more places than me — though that wasn't a surprise. I mean. And she told me where she'd like to go too.

- Oh? Where was that?

- Switzerland, she said. And Australia — or New Zealand. Somewhere far away.

- That was all?

- More or less.

- And did you ask to see her again?

- [no response]

- Did you ask to see her again?

- Of course I did. I thought she liked me.

- But?

- She said that there were other people who'd responded to her ad; people she still wanted to get to know.

- Did that upset you? Did you feel threatened?

- Why should I?

- Being in competition. Thinking you might lose out to someone else; that she might prefer someone other than you.

- [no response]

- Well?

- She said there was this one other guy she quite liked. She was open about it. She had no hesitation in telling me about him. Or shame.

- Don't you think she should have?

- I don't know. It didn't seem right. I mean. Being there with me, and then talking about someone else.

- Is that when you decided you were going to follow her?

§

Faults.

"I find small talk difficult, which usually means I'm quiet when in company. People misunderstand. They mistake it for being moody, disinterested; but I don't think it's that at all. Perhaps I just have a different sense of what's important, significant."

"So this conversation is difficult?"

"I'm prepared to make an exception in your case." The smile was back. I counted that as a win. "So, if ever I go quiet — you know — don't be offended."

"How could I be?" A laugh this time.

"You talked about your parents. Well, my mum died when I was thirteen; since then my dad and I have tolerated each other. Whether you'd call that a fault, I don't know. Depends on your perspective. Anyway, I don't see him much; my choice, but I don't think that bothers him." I paused, waiting for a response. She lifted her beer and took a sip. "Okay, what else? I have a temper of sorts but rarely show it — except when I get *really* moody!" I laughed. "I find it difficult to forgive and forget, though probably expect to be forgiven myself..."

"Dangerous territory." It was an interesting aside.

"Tell me about it. There has been suffering as a result."

"Oh?"

"Later," I smiled, "after you've had your turn."

Again a laugh.

"I find my job a chore and resent having to do it. I suppose I want to feel some kind of privilege, as if I should be excused work, that I should be looked after."

"And do what?" She sought clarification, another cloud briefly passing across her face.

I avoided her question. "Which I guess may make me arrogant, self-centred, and with a misplaced sense of entitlement." This time when I paused it was less to give her the chance to interject, and more to allow the words to sink in. They were intended as a kind of apology in advance.

"Although people might argue I have limited ambition — I don't want to run my own company, for example — I like to think my goals are elsewhere, more 'artistic'. That arrogance, I suppose." I applied the brakes. "How am I doing?"

"Just fine. I may buy you another beer in a minute."

My turn to smile.

"In that case…" I tried to find my rhythm again. "When something goes wrong I can be quick to blame others, even if I know it's my fault. But in those circumstances — hopefully there aren't too many — I'm inclined to stew for a while until I accept culpability."

"And then you apologise?"

"It depends. Sometimes it's too late."

"More dangerous territory!" It was a phrase accompanied by the lifting of her glass from the table. I found myself wondering what kind of poker player she would be.

"Is that enough?"

"Nearly. What about women, girlfriends?"

I was struck by how she separated the question into two categories, as if they might be different; as if she knew that in my case they were.

"Not a stellar track record I suppose — probably down to the aforementioned answers m'Lud — but I think I'm honest enough and I don't cheat."

"And that's a fault?"

"I'm just trying to salvage something from the wreckage!"

She stood and held out her hand for my glass.

"Same again?"

§

- I didn't mean to.

- How can you not mean to follow someone?

- I saw them getting into his car. It was an accident.

- But not an accident that you chose to follow them?

- I was stuck at the traffic lights and there they were across the road. It was an impulse, that's all. I went through the lights and pulled up, then waited. They had to drive past me given the direction his car was facing. It was easy.

- Where did they go?

- Out of town a little way, to the canal. There's a pub not far from that big set of locks.

- *The Boatman*?

- They got out of the car and went into the pub. I waited a few minutes and then went down to the towpath. I could see them. They were sitting outside at one of the tables talking.

- Just like you'd been talking to her in Costa's and in *The Lobster*?

- [no response]

- What then?

- What do you mean?

- What did you do then?

- I just watched. Then she got up and took their empty glasses into the bar. I assumed she was going for a refill so I waited. But she didn't come back out. The guy stood up after a while and went into the pub. I thought he was meeting her inside, so I went back to my car. Then he came out, got in his car, and drove away.

- Alone?

- Yes.

- And where was she?

- Scarpered, I guessed.

- And why might she do that?

- Perhaps she'd decided she didn't like him after all.

- Did you think she might have decided she preferred you?

- [no response]

§

When she didn't return after 10 minutes I went to look for her. Given most of the pub's clientele were enjoying the sunshine, it was oddly quiet inside: only three or four tables occupied, a couple waiting to be served. As I looked their way I noticed two empty glasses at one end of the bar. Of course they could have been anyone's, but I was convinced they were ours — and they were at the end nearest the door, not nearest the toilets.

I went to the bar and asked someone there if they'd seen her and where she went. The barman asked me to describe her — which I was able to do in detail — but to no avail. He was, he said, "too busy to notice anyone". I wasn't sure that made any sense given his job — and considering how beautiful she was.

Just then I saw a lady coming out of the toilets. I went up to her and told her I was looking for my friend, asked if there was anyone else still in the ladies'. She gave me an odd look, but told me it was empty.

Which meant she'd gone. Pretended she was going to get more drinks but had decided to scarper. I wondered if my answers to her question about faults had let me down, if there was something I'd said she didn't like. But I couldn't think of anything. I mean, I'd tried to be as honest as possible given what she'd said about her mum and dad.

For a few moments I stood in the centre of the bar not knowing what to do; then I went outside, into the sunshine, scanned the carpark, then got into my car and drove home.

§

- But that isn't what happened, is it?

- What do you mean?

- All that rubbish about going to *The Lobster*. Lager shandy! You! And they'd never let someone like you in, would they?

- That's rude. I don't know what you mean.

- We'll buy your story about meeting her in Costa, but after that...

- The canal. We went to the canal.

- And she left on her own? Or you didn't see her leave? You expect us to believe that?

- [no response]

§

When I woke up the next morning I knew there was no point trying to call her. Not after what had happened the day before. There's no coming back from something like that is there?

I know I'm not perfect — who is? — but maybe I wasn't perfect enough for her, my faults a little too, well, obtrusive. Where she was so perfect — like a sublimely carved sculpture in a gallery — I was this rough hewn object no-one could be interested in. Perhaps that's what she saw, why she left.

70

§

- Where did you go when you left the canal?

- Home. I told you. I went home.

- Not to your allotment? Quiet there mid-week afternoons, isn't it?

- I went straight home.

- And she didn't want to go with you?

- I said I didn't know where she was.

- That's what you said...

§

I've no idea who could have seen me at the canal with her; I mean, I didn't recognise anyone there. To be honest, I don't know many people. But someone must have seen me because the next day there was a knock on my front door. I could see two large black shapes through the glass panel.

As it happened I already had my shoes on; I had some errands I needed to run, and then a job or two to finish down at the allotment.

I may not have mentioned the allotment. Nor that there was a part of me that had always wanted to ride in a police car.

His Small Existence

He knows from previous experience exactly where Zone F is located — indeed, where all the Zones are — and intends to find a vacant space not far from a shuttle stop. As he drives past packed rows of anonymous BMWs, Audis, and 4x4s standing like soldiers at ease, he catches the tell-tale glimpse of a courtesy bus heading towards the car park exit. No matter how close to a stop he might end up leaving his tax-expensed Mercedes, experience tells him that having just missed one shuttle it will now make sense to walk to the terminal. Doing so is more or less the norm anyway. Looking to the sky, he hopes the rain might hold off a little longer.

Ending up on the edge of Zone E and nowhere near a bus stop, he raises the tailgate on his car, extracts a small suitcase and shoulder bag, then closes the boot. The dull thud of its automated mechanical compression is too familiar, as is the feeling of the car keys in his pocket and the 'beep' when he presses the 'lock' button sight unseen. If he was the kind of man prone to talking to himself, he might indulge in a "here we go again". Instead he merely permits a sigh and checks that he has his passport and boarding card in his jacket pocket. Not being a man who trusts too much in technology, he takes comfort in paper.

By the time he reaches the big roundabout mid-way between the car park and the terminal, two shuttles have passed him and a light drizzle has started. It not being the first time that Sod's Law has played its hand on this particular leg of his journey, he wonders if the inauspicious start might be an ill omen for the flight to Switzerland. Unreliable at the best of times, he is in no mood for it to be delayed today. Wanting to get the journey over and done with has become an increasing priority as the weeks have gone by, that early frisson of excitement in having a contract in an unfamiliar country gradually bleeding away, a little of it lost each time he parks his car, each time the aeroplane lifts off then touches down, each time he squeezes himself onto the bus in Zurich. Getting to know some of the other regulars — even superficially — has been leeching life from him too, that initial feeling of being somehow different to Roger, Dave and Clive replaced by the unwelcome realisation that he is in fact one of them, a member of the clan. It is a family to which he has no desire to be attached, yet one he seemingly cannot avoid.

Hauling his case toward the automatic doors of the terminal, he reminds himself that freedom is within his power, that it has always been so. From nowhere comes a stab of uncertainty. There is a part of him that doesn't want this ritual to end, the part which is always in the ascendant whenever he gets closer to the heartbeat of travelling: the Simon Earnshaw who flourishes his passport and boarding card at the easyJet check-in desk with the air of a man who totally comprehends what is happening; the Simon Earnshaw who slips his shoulder bag onto the x-ray machine and submits himself to the body scanner; the Simon Earnshaw who meanders through the Duty Free shop and thinks of spending money but never does. Duty Free has never been the same since they changed the rules for European Union travellers. This then is the international version of Simon Earnshaw, the one who tries to glory in the fact that he is not a straightforward nine-to-five man; that he isn't someone who commutes from suburb to town and back every day, but one who collects traveller programme points triggering the reward of yet another flight or another night in an anonymous hotel.

As he approaches the departure gate, the bulk of the long antiseptic corridor behind him, he sees Roger and Clive huddled together on the periphery of the milling crowd. Standing near the windows, it is a niche they have come to adopt as their own, one which offers a route to circumvent the bulk of the queue when it comes to boarding. Linked by some sixth sense, they look his way when he is within about thirty metres and watch him all the way to their side as if they might be guiding a plane to rest 'on station'.

Without speaking they nod in unison as he comes to a halt, and Simon Earnshaw — frequent flyer king — glances out of the window onto the familiar pageantry of gangways, fuel trucks, and luggage carriers. Then, setting his small case on its end and slipping the bag from his shoulder, he can't stop himself from again thinking "has it come to this: car park — plane — hotel — office; reverse; repeat?" He tries to remember what the date is — not the day of the week because it can only be a Monday — so he checks the display on his new Apple watch.

"Twenty minutes late," Clive says, misinterpreting the motive behind Simon's action.

"If we're lucky," Roger adds, pessimistically.

Simon has become used to pessimism; it is the constant companion of the regular traveller: there will be an accident on the M62, or the plane will be late, or he won't make it onto the first bus at the other end, or he will have been allocated a room too close to the lift such that the dull purring of its mechanism will stop him from settling to a restful sleep. Not that he ever sleeps well the first night, no matter which room he is given. Nor the second night. Roger and Clive resume their conversation about the weekend's football.

Then an announcement: "easyJet apologises for the delay to its flight…"

The groan is a collective one. Involuntarily half the gathered multitude consult wrists or mobile phones; one or two start tapping messages.

"Thirty-five minutes," he echoes, "could be worse."

It is a feeble attempt to circumvent the dismay; an effort woefully insufficient to prevent Roger's automatic dive into the narrative of horrendous airport experiences, most of which he and Clive have heard more than once. They share a glance. Simon imagines himself taking a blank sheet of paper and drawing a line down its middle, heading the two columns 'what I will miss' and 'what I won't miss'. Perhaps he will do so for real once they are on their way. He determines to put 'waiting' and 'delays' in the second column; then, after a moments further thought, imagines himself appending Roger's name to the same side of the paper.

And two hours later — when they are flying over France, perhaps thirty minutes from beginning their descent — Simon looks at the Filofax sheet sitting ahead of the diary pages for the upcoming week. He has indeed started his list-making and unsurprisingly it is the negative side which is the more significantly populated. Shifting in the too small seat, he tries to move his legs to stop them from going to sleep, then leans just a little to one side in order to try and reclaim at least a portion of the narrow armrest which the traveller to his right laid claim to from the moment he sat down. He wants to add something about fellow passengers to the sheet but refrains from doing so; the man alongside him is close enough to read his jottings, and given everyone seems to speak English, being rude about the people with whom he has to travel doesn't seem worth the risk. At least not yet.

The plus side looks strangely denuded, as if the battle between the two is demonstrably unequal, like a heavyweight taking on a bantamweight; the lighter man is all movement and ineffectual jabs, the larger one replete with devastating upper-cuts. Perhaps when I'm in the hotel, he tells himself — a thought which only goes as far as reminding him all the things he doesn't like about hotels (or at least those budget hotels his contract forces him to stay in): plastic breakfasts, over-priced beer, appalling pillows, lifts that rarely work… As he tries to decide how to encapsulate such a mélange for his sheet, he wonders if Roger were to take on a similar task how long *his* negative list would be. At least A4, if not A3. He is visited by an image of Roger standing at the front of a meeting revealing sheet after sheet of flip chart paper each daubed down one side in red pen, capital letters. All bad. It is a vision which makes him smile, and he wonders for a brief moment whether he had been a little premature in putting Roger's name in the negative column.

And what of Clive? He isn't in Roger's league when it comes to moaning or complaining, but if you wound him up he could chunter away with the best of them. Yet there is something a little more measured about Clive. Perhaps it is because he hasn't been on this haul for quite as long, or because he is the more senior man. Simon also likes to imagine Clive harbouring a secret life away from work, the airports and the hotels; that he has a few more delicate strings to his bow, hobbies to elevate him above what he appears to be at thirty-two thousand feet. A passion for opera, perhaps; or a part-time archaeologist. If that were the case then it would surely be reason enough to be generous when it came to deciding where Clive sat on his sheet. But without the evidence? There is a fence upon which to be sat.

And what if Roger and Clive were undertaking an identical exercise and happened to look his way?

He likes to think their instinct would be to immediately add his name to the positive column. Isn't he a 'good egg', someone who helps pass the time when needed, who has the odd story to inform or entertain? What could they say about him to his detriment? He is not — by his own assessment at least — a bore, a bigot, a chauvinist, or a racist; he is even-handed, loves his family; he likes a beer and a joke as well as the next man... Nothing there to count against him. Perhaps he has been a little grumpy of late, moaning about the commute, how inane his job is, how he longs for the end of his contract. But that is all par for the course, normal banter for part-time ex-pats like him and Roger and Clive. He hasn't told them about his plan, the letter he has in his bag, the intention to hand it to his boss in the morning. And if he had, how might he respond when Roger and Clive — having dissected that self same plan and challenged the financial wisdom of executing it — pressed him about what was to follow? "What will you do when there's no M62 to tackle, no dragging of luggage from the car park, no squeezing onto the bus at the other end, no hotel on expenses?" Would he be honest? And if so, how might that — both his decision to resign and his lack of planning as to what came after — affect his location on their binary lists? He suspects Roger might say one thing and think another; outwardly he'd be all gusto and "well done, mate!", but privately think he was an idiot. Only one side of the line to go after that. And Clive? Simon likes to think that Clive would be more considered and assume that there was something else — personal, emotional, more important — driving the decision. Perhaps he might have been thinking of doing the same thing himself, freeing up his time for his beloved opera. Perhaps Simon's radical move might just prove inspirational enough to give him the push *he* needed. On the plus side then.

A fifty-fifty split after all.

Florian, Simon's boss, is a different animal entirely. Were he the type of person to entertain the idea of such a list, whatever he placed in the negative column would reside there for the shortest amount of time possible before he swept it away. And should something exist in the rarified atmosphere of the positive, he would strive to find a way of making it irrelevant. Florian is a man who likes to rub things out. According to his own credo he is dynamic, always on the move, a man with a well-earned reputation: straight talking, often to the point of rudeness; not one to dither over a decision; single-minded and laser-focussed. If he regarded himself as being a man on a mission, he expected everyone else in his demesne to be on that mission with him. This was the way he ran his teams, his function. He expected his ethos to be their ethos. Behind his back, most of his staff had nicknames for him; perhaps it was his part-Austrian ancestry which had given rise to 'The Fürher' — though only from the small British contingent. And in secret too. At least that was the theory.

Simon had tried to like him. From day one he told himself that he should appreciate Florian's directness: it was great knowing where you stood, what was expected of you; even when you had fallen short. On occasion he had seen Florian let down his guard — usually after a few glasses of wine — but more frequently watched him let fly at a colleague who had let him down. In Florian's world business *was* personal.

"What the fuck's this?"

Simon had left his resignation letter in Florian's in-tray at the beginning of the day and then embarked upon his usual round of Tuesday morning team meetings with the leaders of the three groups he looked after. He had asked Alicia for a slot in Florian's diary toward the end of the day — "half-an-hour should do it" — yet had been hauled out of his ten o'clock and frog-marched into Florian's office. His letter lays open on the desk; Florian is standing behind it, back to the window, facing the door. The explosion comes before Simon is fully into the room. The door not quite closed, Florian's words could not have gone unheard in the corridor.

"I know it's sudden, Florian, but I just can't do it any more."

"Can't do what, exactly?"

"The travelling; the time away from home. It was fun, exciting for a while…"

"Fun?" Florian spears the word at him. "You aren't here to have 'fun'. We don't pay you so that you can have 'fun'."

"I know that."

"We pay you to get results, Simon. That's all. That's the deal." Florian glances at the letter. "You have a contract for another two months. Are you telling me you are not going to honour that?"

"I was hoping we could negotiate something…"

"Why should I? Tell me that. It's not as if your results have been so stellar that we can't manage without you. They haven't been. Average at best."

Simon looks down at the letter suddenly wondering what he had actually said in it. Had his words betrayed him?

"Average at best. Shit." Repeating himself, Florian turns away and looks out of the window. Legend has it that saying 'shit' is Florian's way of buying all the time he needs to make a decision. In the street below a tram makes its way towards the station. "What do you expect me to do? There are ways to make things happen," he turns away from the window and looks at his desk again, points, "and this is not one of them. There are directors in this building who would try and persuade you to stay, or offer to increase your day rate. Is that what you expect of me?"

"No." Simon shakes his head, painfully and acutely aware that he has no idea what he was expecting — other than something more civilised.

"Get out, Simon."

"Yes, Florian." Simon says somewhat obsequiously, then turns towards the door.

"And I don't mean my office. I'm not releasing you to go back to your little meetings, or to your over-large inbox stuffed with unread emails. I mean, get out: of your desk, the office, this building. I've asked Alicia to cancel your hotel and your return flight. If you want to be free then you are. Get your things together then find your own way home."

§

His wait at the airport has ticked beyond three hours. It had taken him less than ten minutes to gather his few personal items from his desk and then walk to the building's exit leaving his pass at the reception desk. At the hotel he verified that his room had been cancelled before repacking the clothes he had unpacked less than twenty-four hours previously. The bus to the airport was oddly quiet; there were no faces he recognised.

"I'm afraid the mid-day flight is full, but we do have space on the four o-clock."

He had taken the only practical option available to him and paid an inflated price for his seat. Facing immediate inconvenience and expense had not been part of his plan — as much as he'd had one. He had foreseen just one sequence of events triggered by his letter: a civilised conversation later that afternoon; agreement as to a revised timetable for his departure; the shaking of hands. Florian's hair-trigger explosion hadn't figured anywhere.

When Simon's personal phone pings, he remembers with a pang leaving the work Blackberry on his desk along with his laptop. His old desk. He recalls the walk to the elevators, conscious of the eyes following him. The phone bears a message from Laurent, one of his team members: *I just heard. Shit.* Same word, different meaning.

How should he respond? He wonders about trying to explain, to use Laurent as a conduit for his version of the truth. But he decides there is no point; not only would it be an unfair burden on Laurent — if not a career-limiting one — he, like everyone else, will soon get the official version via Florian, and once that has happened no other interpretation will be countenanced. He types *Yes, it happens* then presses 'send'.

Given it is nearly three o'clock, Simon knows his fellow passengers will begin to appear soon enough. What kind of people take a mid-afternoon flight to Manchester on a Tuesday? He imagines business people heading for a Wednesday morning meeting with the aim of flying back the same afternoon; or civilians visiting family; or perhaps a few bound for a short holiday in the North West. Being so close to the mountains here, he wonders how strong the lure of the English Lakes could possibly be for Swiss natives. In the same way as he had started his good-bad list on the way out, he tries to compare Lucerne with Kendal or Keswick then gives up. A frivolous exercise.

Before he started work in Switzerland he had talked to Fran about them taking a holiday: "take advantage of me being in

Zurich" he had said. And now he knows he will have to deliver an entirely different message. She is not expecting him home until late on Friday, instead of which he will walk through the door around about the time the kids are going to bed. Three days early. Turmoil will ensue. For a moment he wonders whether it might be prudent to delay his arrival until she is home alone, and calls up a hotel booking website on his phone to see how much Manchester Airport hotels would charge him for one night. Prices are extortionate, and when he adds that potential cost to what he has already committed for the flight, he imagines money disappearing lemming-like from his bank account. Not only that, but there is the corollary of nothing now going into it for a while.

He propels himself forward. Tomorrow morning; back on the job-hunting treadmill. How long had it taken him last time? Commuting to Europe had been an option of last resort, and since then there has been nothing in the UK economy to suggest things will have changed for the better. Simon realises that to some extent the immediacy of job-hunting will be of secondary concern. Although her outward reaction is likely to suggest otherwise, Fran's response to his change of circumstance could be even more extreme than Florian's. Simon knows she will instantly translate it into what it means for her, the children. There will be questions. If "what about that holiday?" is one of the first, he knows he will have escaped lightly. Weighing up such a likelihood, optimism leaks from him and he closes the hotel app, resigned to facing the music sooner rather than later. Better to get both explosions over in one day.

And then: "easyJet apologises for the delay to its flight to Manchester…"

Macchiato and Motive

A small circular tray. On it, two cups of coffee — one black, one white — and a small cream plate on which, laying on its side, is a single slice of Victoria sponge. Along with the tray, she holds two forks and two paper serviettes in one of her hands. Once the tray is on the compact table, she places the black coffee in front of him, the white in front of where she will sit, the plate between them. Opening her handbag she removes a small plastic bottle, extracts a single tablet from it, then places it alongside his coffee. Then she hands him a serviette and a fork; rests the now empty tray against one of the table legs; sits down. With a certainty that can only come from practice, she divides the wedge into two using her own fork, rotates the plate so that the largest chunk is facing him. Then she takes a small forkful from her own partial slice and puts the morsel into her mouth.

All this is done wordlessly.

While he has been waiting, while she has been engaged in purchase, deployment and division, his head has been bent, eyes apparently fixed on a spot in the centre of the table. One might be forgiven for thinking he is suffering from some kind of physical restriction — unable to lift his head or straighten his neck — until the moment he sees the pill, the instant she begins to eat, as if these are triggers, a release which gives his body energy. 'Plugged-in' as it were, he is suddenly animated: he pops the pill into his mouth and takes the merest sip of coffee; attacks his own part-slice; says something in a register too low to be heard even on the next table. You get the sense of him resuming a conversation after a forced intermission.

The routine is a well-worn one. The barista may not know their names nor where they are from, but she now recognises their unvarying order and now has sufficient familiarity to be able to engage the elderly woman in conversations about the weather or the busyness of the café — though it is most often the elder who makes reference to how few tables are free or how noisy the children in the far corner are being in spite of the crayons they grasp and the pictures they are attempting to colour-in. If, in listening to these complaints the barista thinks she is merely doing her job then she underestimates her importance. The old woman and her husband are regulars in the bookshop café partly because they are treated with respect, like human beings. Had she been able to eavesdrop on their conversation, more than once the barista would have heard the woman compliment her, the friendliness and consideration shown. In its own way, the relationship is a symbiotic one.

"Your favourite old cronies in again?" asks the manager rhetorically from over her shoulder.

Having already learned he is not expecting an answer — and compounded by her taking an increasing dislike to him — she says nothing, smiles at the next customer, pushes on. These days she is constantly aware of the distance between them, a distance difficult to maintain in the cramped space behind the counter. More than once in recent weeks he has brushed past her when he hadn't needed to, allowed his fingers to touch hers in an 'accidental' attempt to grab the same plate, the same cup. She may still be young, but she has enough friends who work in similar places — friends armed with anecdotes and warnings — to know where this might lead. But she doesn't want conflict, she just wants to do her job. She is happy working here — and she needs the money.

At the table next to the elderly couple a young man looks up from his laptop screen. Freeing his hands from the keyboard, he reaches for his juice, takes a sip. He has perfected the art of making a single drink last over an hour. It is a means of securing his place, to prevent them from kicking him out. Liking it here, surrounded by the aura of books, he has found it a productive place to work — and anything that even marginally mitigates the struggle attendant on writing his thesis is to be welcomed!

When he first tried the bookshop café he drank coffee; but finding one cup bought him no more than thirty minutes, in order to stay longer he was compelled to buy a second. It was a tactic which soon enough proved financially unsustainable. Hence the juice. He recognises the barista not merely from his regular presence there, but from the university; he has seen her around the campus and although they have not spoken outside the boundaries of the café, he hopes their tenuous connection gifts him just a little extra 'free time' when she is on duty. Other than to order his drinks, not making any additional effort to speak to her is easy enough to rationalise: she is often busy and he is always shy. Especially with girls. His little experience thus far has already proved disastrous, not merely from the rollercoaster he had been put through emotionally, but in the aftermath. Indeed he still finds himself in turmoil from time to time, especially when he sees the young woman concerned — or her friends — in the refectory or library. Hence the café is an oasis for a secondary reason. He tells himself there is time enough ahead for the trauma of emotional entanglement, and that what matters now is the final push on his thesis and getting his Ph.D. After that he can move on, even if he has no firm idea where he might be 'moving on' to. The university has been making noises about keeping him on as a junior lecturer; there is a module — not quite aligned to his specialism — he could teach. And later on? Well, he'd see how things went.

He finds himself wondering about the old couple and if they ever faced a time when they'd had to 'see how things went'. Perhaps when they first met each other, or later when they married, had children. Perhaps they are in the midst of such a situation now. Witnessing the proffering of the pill, he imagines the man being unwell and his wife saying "well, we'll just have to see how things go". Although he has come to recognise them, he too doesn't know them; yet in spite of that, finds himself hoping the medical scenario doesn't apply.

Before going back to his keyboard, he glances up, sees the barista looking his way. Recognition; then she goes back to work.

In the far corner there is a shout from one of the two children, upset that their sibling is keeping one of the crayons for themselves. At a table mid-way between them and the student, two women break off from their conversation and look toward the offending child. Theirs is a shared look of distain, as if they couldn't possibly be associated with anything as demeaning as children. Yet they are both edging towards their fifties — even if they are trying not to show it — and have suffered the indignities of childbirth, the unfair suffering attendant on the raising of offspring. But now they find themselves free: in one case because her husband is often away overseas with work and their sons are elsewhere, a trainee barrister and a junior officer in the army; for the other, freedom has come at the cost of one failed marriage, a collapsing second one, and a daughter who has proven so difficult to handle that her decision to go to a university miles away in some remote part of Scotland came as something of a godsend.

Between them, they feel as if they have the whole gamut of negative adult experiences well and truly covered, though the pleasure of being able to sit having coffee with each other —

friends reunited, as it were — is meagre reward for their endurance. If you asked each of them in private however, they might confess that 'friendship' could be pushing it a little, especially when one considers this and that... The friction between them, albeit camouflaged when in public like this, is evidenced through subtle competition and a desperation to emphasise any possible sign of superiority: the better shoes, the newest hairstyle, the more refined make-up, the latest triumph. This surface ambition is also manifestation of a desire to return to who they once were — young like the barista, perhaps — not who they are now. In their conversation — voices raised a little louder than they need to be — there is an edge, the need to have the last word, score the most points.

On the table furthermost from the counter, two men sit and observe the scene. The elder of the two, slightly careworn, fidgets in his chair; his nicotine patches failing to work, he is desperate to be back outside so that he can have another cigarette.

"Don't you find these places fascinating," the younger man asks.

"What?"

"Cafés."

"Why fascinating?"

"Because of what you can see, what you can observe. 'All life is here'; isn't that the quote?"

"I wouldn't know about that," says the older man dismissively. He scans the room. "But I suppose you're right: all sorts of people, all sorts of stories, all sorts of possibilities."

The younger man looks back to him. "Possibilities?"

"Aye." The other allows his native Scots accent to broaden for effect. "Possibilities."

"Such as?"

"Criminal intent. Or even past criminal deeds."

"Criminal!" The younger man laughs.

"You can scoff if you want to, lad, but when you've been in the force as long as I have, seen what I've seen…"

This boasting has been a recurrent theme of their short professional relationship, a kind of showing-off punctuated by myths and legends, only some of which the junior partner believes to be true.

"And here?"

"Murder." Now the older man has found a theme, the fidgeting has stopped.

"Murder?"

"Any one of them." The senior officer waves an arm in the general direction of the other tables. "All could have cause. Like the barista who hates her boyfriend or her boss. Or that long-haired guy at the computer; probably frustrated in love or something."

"And the old couple?"

"Mercy killing. One of them has been given a terminal diagnosis and the other wants to limit their suffering. Very likely. Or the father who's just about had enough of his kids and is planning their 'accident'. Or the women who really can't stand each other — especially the one who suspects the other of having an affair with her husband… Murder, everywhere you look."

"And your experience tells you that any one of these people could be a killer?"

"It does."

And as it transpires — and somewhat bizarrely — eventually he is proved right…

The Guide at Fountain's Abbey

He liked the early mornings best, when it was still quiet, before they let the public in. It had become a ritual. "We need you to go down to the Abbey," they'd said on his first day, "and do a quick recce, just to check." He'd asked them what he was checking for. "Anomalies." Maureen had seen the confusion flicker in his face. "You know, to confirm that no-one's got in over night — human or animal — and that, if there's been any heavy rain or strong winds, the old place has stood up okay." He doubted whether, after all these years, a spot of rain was going to do any damage.

Once he'd settled in, he started to get to work slightly earlier in order to give himself a little more time on his rounds. He had a deadline by which he needed to report back, so any form of loitering was out of the question. If he wanted to spend more time in the Abbey — as he found he did — he had to do so at his own expense. During those first few weeks he began to arrive five minutes early, then ten, and so on. Settling into his new routine — and with his fellow colleagues getting used to him and his ways — by the time Christmas came his penchant for extended inspections became something of a soft joke with the rest of the team. "You must know every brick," one of them said. "Not yet," he replied. When they closed the monument for Christmas Day, that was hard.

Not having been a particularly young man when he started, getting down to the Abbey during the winter became increasingly problematic, especially after he slipped one February morning and banged his head because he'd not been looking where he was going, mesmerised — as always! — by the sunlight through the old window arches. After that, they let him use the buggy on mornings when he was feeling particularly stiff. When he took it, he did so reluctantly.

It was early during the Spring solstice when he found the monk waiting for him. Emerging from the darkness of the Frater of the Lay Brothers he had initially missed the other man standing near the wall of the Chapter House, his eyes taking a moment to re-adjust to the growing brightness of the day. He loved the long vaulted dark frater; for him it felt like the heart of the Abbey, the peaceful place where he always started his rounds. It grounded him, provided him with the context for his day. Perhaps more than that. The monk, simply dressed in long brown vestments was, he realised, looking directly towards him. No-one had mentioned there would be someone else doing the rounds; perhaps it was a new colleague, an actor rehearsing a part, pandering to the trend for 'interactive experiences'. None the wiser — and keen to get off on the right foot — he made his way round the cloister towards the Chapter House.

"Morning," he called from perhaps twenty or thirty yards away, "looks like it will be a grand day."

His companion said nothing. Getting closer, he saw the monk was older than he had first thought, and surely too old to be a new recruit to the team unless his ageing was the genius of make-up.

"I've not seen you before," he offered, trying to find a way into conversation. Getting no reply, he glanced around the cloister, up to the external walls of the nave, and over the monk's shoulder into the darkness of the Chapter House. "It's so peaceful here isn't it?"

It was the kind of gambit he used when he came across visitors during the day, liking to address those who stood slightly apart from the rest, standing in quiet contemplation. There was never any answer other than 'yes' — except this time.

The monk turned and walked through the passage alongside the Chapter House and towards the main edifice of the abbey, the presbytery, the nave. And so he walked with him, commenting not just on the physicality of the place but how it made him feel. In reality it was a one-sided conversation, though it didn't seem that way. Pausing by the north transept, he found himself looking up at the broken walls to where the roof would have been, and to the deepening blue sky beyond. He stood there for a moment, then when he returned his gaze to ground level he found he was alone.

Back in the office, he asked Maureen whether they were planning any new features for visitors. "Features?" she had asked, "Such as?" "Oh, I don't know, a more interactive version of the tours we currently offer." She had laughed gently at his use of the word 'interactive' as if it belonged to a generation alien to him. He let it go. Then after a pause, she said "Are you okay?" Confused, he sought clarification. "Why?" "You look a little pale, that's all." He let that go too.

The next morning — arriving even earlier than usual — it was with some impatience he made his way down to the Abbey, heading immediately for the Chapter House. Disappointed not to find the monk there, he resumed his normal routine — only to find the brown-robed figure waiting for him in the Refectory. Not expecting any verbal acknowledgement, he merely nodded to the monk who this time nodded in recognition. Just then he felt a slight chill which, once it had passed, permitted them to begin their slow inspection together, disappearing side-by-side into the darkness of the Frater of the Lay Brothers.

Southmead Road

"You could chop off my legs and I'd still love you."

"Yeah, right."

"But best not put it to the test, eh?" I released her from my hug.

"Look Dad," she said impatiently, "I'm in a hurry; I need to be on station in fifteen minutes."

"I'll walk with you."

"If you think you can keep up!"

"I'm not that old and decrepit yet!"

When she set off, I had to jog the first few paces.

"What's 'on station' mean, anyway?"

"It means I have to be in my uniform and ready to serve customers. One minute late and they dock some of my wages."

"Sounds harsh," I suggested.

"Yeah — but no-one's late."

We walked on for a few more paces.

"I thought I might try working again," I said.

She laughed at the notion. "You hate work, Dad. You're useless at it — and you don't need to do it anyway."

At times like this Cath reminded me of her mother. She liked to think she was spiky, but underneath she was as soft as jelly.

"Thanks for the vote of confidence."

"I didn't mean that." She aimed a fake punch at my arm without breaking stride. "But give me an example of a job you were able to put your heart and soul into… That's what I mean. For as long as I can remember all you were ever doing was going through the motions."

"I didn't realise it was so obvious — or you'd be able to see that when you were a child."

"Well, I'm your child, Dad. Yours and Mum's. Being able to see things is in the genes."

I couldn't deny that — not could I deny her when, after a few strides more, she insisted she leave me behind. "Unless you want to make up the shortfall in my pay?" It was an empty threat because she knew I would do so if she asked — and because there was no way she would let it come to that. Moderating my pace, I watched her gallop away. In addition to her general fieriness, there was something of Sue in Cath's stride; in fact since Sue had gone I was seeing more and more of her in our daughter. Perhaps that's only natural; and perhaps it was why recently I had been pestering her more and more. She didn't seem to mind; I think she took it for what it was, saw through me. What was it she'd said? "Being able to see things is in the genes."

If anyone were to challenge Cath's theory based on what they knew of me, I'd defend the hypothesis by arguing that Sue's genes were the dominant ones in our child-making collaboration; indeed, as evidence, I could point to her track record as an historian, her articles and lectures. She'd had a knack of being able to sift through the concrete, the proven, and get to the softer underbelly of history. To any who might persist in their challenge, I'd lay claim to nothing more than a supporting role — especially as history was a blind spot for me. I tended to find the factual difficult — which undoubtedly contributed to my problem in holding down a steady job. It was never that I couldn't do the work, but rather that I found it difficult to focus on the tasks given me, or see the value in them. In those general topics where I could never quite get the point, Sue had been able to dig and delve, to go beneath the surface. She could — I often told her — be interested in anything as long as it had a past to be uncovered. She would have made a great archaeologist.

To be honest I wasn't really thinking of finding a new job. It was something I'd wanted to tease Cath with, just to get a reaction — and one which proved delightfully predictable. She was correct in that I didn't need to work: it was the blessing of insurance policies — their curse being the circumstances which required you to claim against them. As far as "seeing's in the genes" was concerned, it was a topic we'd debated before Sue died, the three of us. Cath would put forward a new and always benevolent hypothesis about me at which point Sue would delve into my past in order to prove or disprove it, and I — outnumbered and outgunned — always ended up playing a rather weak defensive hand. "My gift," I once told them, "if you want to call it that, is actually the complete opposite to being able to see things. It's because I *can't* see facts or what's in front of my face — politics, culture, you name it — that I have to make things up. And making things up has nothing to do with 'seeing'." But they'd shot that one down too. "Kid yourself as much as you like, Darling," — I remember Sue putting a hand on my arm — "but the only way you're able to write your stories, create your worlds, is because you see what's going on in *this* one. And because you don't care for it, you're replacing it with realms and lives you *do* care about."

Even as I protested, I knew they were more right than wrong. Whatever my source, motivation or talent, I had established a reputation as a minor author, mainly short stories, predominately 'speculative fiction'. It used to annoy Sue if, within her earshot, anyone suggested I was 'just a sci-fi writer'. Like me, she hated sci-fi; unlike us, Cath loved it. Perhaps it was a generational thing. In any event, Cath was right, I didn't need to work for money; nor did I need to work to compensate for any kind of internal emptiness or emotional shortfall. At least that was *my* specious theory! Cath pointed out that I had a job in any case — my writing — if only I would take it seriously. Since she'd been about fourteen, that was a drum she'd joined Sue in banging. Now she was the family soloist she seemed to enjoy crashing her fist against it with even greater vigour. It was a rhythm that both annoyed and invigorated me, even after listening to it for many years.

From time to time I thought it cheeky that Cath should want to get into a debate with me about working. Three years at York and a subsequent First Class degree, and there she was, donning a polyester uniform most days of the week to serve shit food to customers, the majority of whom wouldn't have known *good* food if they ran over it in the car park. An unlikely scenario, I'll admit. "It's only temporary, dad," she'd say on those rare occasions I'd challenge her (drum-banging not being my thing), "until I decide what the next right step is." She'd had options: the offer of a post-grad place; two graduate intake schemes from big multi-nationals; three friends who'd gone off to travel Europe for twelve months and had wanted her to go with them. But here she was, back at home babysitting me. Sue's death presumably had something to do with it, bad timing and all that. Perhaps she thought I wouldn't cope; perhaps *I* was her project, at least for the next few months. I used to watch her go off to work and blame myself for my own inadequacies, frailties, and apparent lack of independence. Then, during other moments of weakness and self-pity, I'd blame Sue for leaving us — for leaving me — in such a state. Joke or not, I'm sure a psychologist would say my suggestion about getting a job had nothing to do with work and everything to do with trying to demonstrate that I was okay, had things under control, and that it was fine for Cath to go off and live her own life. Except in Cath's eyes all such nonsense did was to demonstrate just what a hopeless case I was, and added fuel to the fire as to why she needed to be there to look after me. Sometimes I wondered just who the parent in our relationship was.

She was out of sight in no time, which allowed me to pause at the corner of Avenue Road and then take a left into the rectangle that was Southmead Park. Walking diagonally across it to the entrance at the far corner, I emerged onto Southmead Road opposite its small parade: two charity shops, a mini-supermarket, a somewhat shabby carpet shop, a place that sold nuts and dried fruit, one newsagent, an old fashioned gents outfitters, a bookmakers, and an estate agents. Nine businesses, their combined facades now an all too familiar sight. Had I been any kind of artist I think I might have been able to draw the entire row from memory with my eyes closed. And in excruciating detail. Which in a way I was, though with words rather than pencil lines or brushstrokes. If I was Cath's project, then Southmead Road — and it's little parade of shops — was mine.

This particular day it was the turn of the bookmaker's, 'Willie's Wagers'. When I walked through the door, the bell gave its usual tired 'ping'. At the counter Sashi and Harv looked up to see who had dared to disturb their peace and quiet. Not that the place was empty. To my left, two men sat on stools examining cards for the dog-racing later that morning and, nearer the counter, Jim stood mesmerised at one of the fruit machines, his hand feeding it coins as if he were the keeper at some bizarre kind of zoo, the animal needing to be fed to be kept alive. I knew them all. A bit like all the shops, 'Willie's Wagers' had undoubtedly seen better days, presumably when the eponymous 'Willie' had run the place — though I'd struggled to find any record of or reference to any such individual.

"Morning chaps," I said when I reached the counter. They nodded. "Any news?"

Harv glanced at Sashi as if seeking approval to proceed.

"Couple of near misses, that's about it."

"Of note?"

"A chap was half-a-length away from picking up twenty grand: the last one in his acca got pipped in the final half furlong."

"Wow." I feigned being impressed but it was a story I'd heard numerous times before. "Do we know him?" I spoke as if I was a member of staff — which, at times, was how they'd come to treat me.

Harv shook his head.

"Don't think he was local," Sashi clarified.

I nodded.

"Well…" I said, deliberately vaguely, then headed to the stool waiting for me in my usual position. It was a station along the front wall which gave me a decent enough view of the shop, the comings and goings through the door. I pulled a blue notebook from the bag I'd been carrying — the one with 'Willie's' written in thick permanent pen on the cover — and opened it.

I'm not exactly sure when I had the idea about the Southmead shops. It would have been after Sue had died, and after Cath had reestablished herself at home. Perhaps it had come in a dream or while I was out walking. Maybe it had always been there and I'd needed an excuse to give it a go. What it felt like of course — in addition to being a job! — was both a tribute and a challenge. I had decided to try and depict the lives of these shops — their staff and their customers — as accurately and as concretely as I possibly could. I wanted to find out if I could indeed 'see' facts, if I could observe things in the way Sue used to. So I set myself the challenge of doing just that, the intention being that there should be no invention, nothing speculative or unreal, simply what I saw and heard. As if I was a witness to something. Life, I suppose. There was an element of Georges Perec about the endeavour: *Life — A User's Manual*, set in Southmead Road.

In terms of cooperation, some of the shops had been easier to convince than others. Being a little bit known helped. The charity shops, assuming my presence and project would bring them publicity, were the first on-board; then, once I'd started to build some momentum, the others gradually fell into line. The Estate Agent was particularly difficult to persuade, and it took an age to get 'Willie's Wagers' signed-up. I would cycle through the emporia trying to spend time in each of them once a week, usually on the same day. Wednesday was 'Willie's Wagers' day; it seemed appropriate, all those W's. In each establishment I'd found myself a suitable perch, made sure I was out of the way, then started making notes in a dedicated book. It was, I reflected, 'seeing' with a capital 'S'. Now, some weeks into my experiment, my notebooks were beginning to fill. I had told myself that as soon as I'd used up all the space in one of them then that would be it, end of experiment.

And then what?

It was a question which had been preoccupying me for a little while. My initial idea had been to take a break — possibly even go away for a few days — and then come back to the notebooks as 'cold' as possible to see what I had. At that point there would be options. I could indeed don a Perec-like mantle and turn my notes into an unvarnished look at 'normal' suburban life. Or I could revert to my natural style and create a speculative world based on what I'd seen, see the life of Southmead Road through a 'magic realism' lens. I could choose to insert myself fully into the narratives and make them as much about me as anyone else — or do the opposite. Or I could choose to do nothing at all with what I'd written, satisfied that I had proven a point about my ability to 'see', not only to me and Cath, but to Sue too. But doing nothing felt like turning traitor on the people I'd spent the last number of weeks with; in many ways the Sashis and Harvs were as invested in my project as much as I — except they didn't know it.

Which is why I'd walked part-way with Cath this morning, because the upcoming visit to 'Willie's Wagers' was going to result in me filling the last pages in their blue notebook. As it now has. I'd wanted to find out if — by me making that lame gag about getting a job — she might unknowingly offer me a clue as to the appropriate destiny of all that material, ten multi-coloured books filled with 'seeing'.

As I head back across the park at the end of my short working day, I know for certain a number of things: I won't be going back to any of the Southmead Road shops any time soon; my new friends — like Sashi and Harv — are unlikely to see me much again; but most importantly, I now have a growing urge to push on, to turn my scrappy notes into something more important. But I won't be doing that today. Today I have to prepare a special dinner for Cath and I; a kind of celebration. It will take her by surprise — as will the reason I've done it. She'll be suspicious, of course; perhaps she'll imagine I'm about to break the news of a new woman in my life, so I won't be able to dawdle. And so I'll need to show her a selection from the drafts I have produced, and then ask her the big question: "what do you think mum would say?"

§

in Cancer Research

It's not just the stock and fittings that are 'used'; the clientele often seem second-hand too. Occasionally someone more glamorous will cross the threshold as if they've taken the wrong exit off a film set. They wander between the meagre clothes' rails appearing somewhat lost, before smiling apologetically at no-one in particular then beating a retreat.

❋

I wonder about that phrase 'pre-owned' — a modern, politically-correct term I suppose — and whether or not you might be able to apply it to people. If you can, does that make *me*, as a widower, 'pre-owned'? Or would it only apply to those whose relationships had collapsed? Or from which they had been freed? The latter — with the suggestion of release — seems more fitting. Not that I've any idea what such freedom must feel like, the slipping from the ownership of someone; perhaps it's like an escape from slavery. My own slavery was benevolent and willingly entered into, entirely self-inflicted — which presumably makes it something different. Perhaps the dividing line between dedication and slavery is thinner than we might imagine.

❋

I watch couples as they come into the shop to browse, watch them expose the generic patterns to which they almost invariably conform. The woman (assuming a heterosexual couple) is usually the more 'aggressive' shopper; the man tends to take a step back, 'sham browsing' in the shadows. He's really only killing time until he gets the signal which releases him back onto Southmead Road. Perhaps he has aspirations elsewhere: 'Walter & Smyth' or 'Willie's'. You usually get a good idea as to which of the two by how furtively the male browses and how he is dressed: specimens who favour a bookmakers over a gents' outfitters tend to be a world apart!

*

Most people refer to it as 'The Cancer Shop' as if it were the place to go and buy the disease, rather than somewhere raising funds to eradicate it.

"100 grams of cancer please, and a bag of sherbet lemons."

Would you buy it in grams? Or perhaps in lumps, like sugar.

*

"What are you doing?"

"Writing," I answer, allowing an inquisitive woman space to articulate a suitable response. She pauses for a moment, clearly thinking, then surprises me with her answer.

"Better than taking photographs, I suppose."

I suspect most people would tend to agree, even if they weren't sure why they were doing so.

*

Because Southmead Road is such a short parade of shops it's perhaps inevitable that individuals frequent more than one of them during a single visit. And although you could be excused for assuming that those who visit the Cancer Shop are also likely to entertain the hospice shop too, I discover this is not the case. Yes, there are those who browse in both either because they are looking for something specific or because that is their way; yet it is surprising the percentage who remain loyal to one or the other. They will have their reasons of course; after all, not everyone has been touched in some way by cancer or feels compelled to lend their support here.

Less surprising are the overlaps — or lack of them — between other combinations of shop. But overall, how many people are in the super-set of Southmead regulars? More than fifty? Less than a hundred?

Take Reg. He was in here about twenty minutes ago. Dapper old gent. According to Jen he's been pursuing the same routine, day after day, ever since his Delia died. No excuses, no variation. Perhaps that's his way of keeping her alive, continuing to do alone that which they had always done together. Reg is a jigsaw man. He walks in, goes straight up to the jigsaw shelf, looks, then comes over to the counter. "Got any new ones in?" he'll ask either Jen or Marge. He knows there may be some in the sorting room upstairs which have not yet made it down to the shop. Sometimes they'll go and look, either because they're not sure or because they want to humour him. When the answer is 'no' — as it most often is — Reg will return to the jigsaw shelf and reappraise those currently available. Unless he decides to plump for one he has already rejected (which happens infrequently) after a few minutes he will turn and meander back through the shop and out onto the street.

Having seen me there often enough — and in the hospice shop too as he follows the same routine — Reg and I have progressed through nodding recognition to 'good morning' or 'good afternoon'. One day he asked me what I was doing, so I told him. It didn't really seem to register. Maybe Reg is the kind of person who responds best to pictures and images.

~

in the Daffodil Hospice Shop

There is an odd kind of calm that pervades 'Daffodil's'. Yes, it has that vaguely musty smell attendant on most charity shops — a combination of mothballs, dust, and old lives — but there is something else too; perhaps a kind of reverence or respect. And perhaps because it is not part of 'a chain' in the way the Cancer shop could be seen, its patrons feel they can have a different relationship with it.

It's difficult to put your finger on.

❉

I've not timed it so this analysis is unscientific, but I think people spend more time in 'Daffodil's' than the Cancer shop. On average. It's an impression, nothing more. I wonder if there's something less 'transactional' about 'Daffodil's'. Or less 'commercial'.

❉

Today a man asked me what I was doing there and so, as I always do, I told him. He responded by telling me about his father who had been a resident at the hospice for the last two months of his life. Whilst he refrained from too many personal details, he was full of praise for the staff there, was keen for me to know what he felt. I think he'd assumed that I would be producing some kind of PR for them.

Which, in a way, I suppose I might be.

~

in Willie's Wagers

There's one regular Harv calls 'the great unwashed' — and with good reason. Maybe he saves the experience of a bath for a birthday treat. You don't want to get downwind of him — which in the case of 'Willie's' means anywhere within about twelve feet. If he comes anywhere near me I immediately find an excuse to go and talk to Sashi.

Is it significant no-one has bothered to find out his name?

There's a history there; there must be. He'd be the kind of project who would have fascinated Sue — but I doubt even she would have been able to overcome the smell.

Dedication to a cause can only take you so far.

~

in Six 'til Eight

At the far end of the store Dee has had one of those little video screens installed. It's perched on the top shelf in the small homeware section and prattles on all day about super-glue or some such. An endless loop.

Even at the front of the shop where I've been allowed to perch (a small stool at one end of the counter, neither in the shop nor apart from it) the screen's audio occasionally drifts this way. None of the words being distinguishable at this distance, it's more a drone than anything else — but having

109

been here so often I can still tell exactly where they are in the advert.

＊

Unsurprisingly, of all the stores on Southmead Road, 'Six 'til Eight' has the most volatile clientele. Or do I mean dynamic, transient? It's the kind of place where people 'pop in' for things: the bread they forgot to buy, an extra pint of milk, some sandwiches to go and eat in the park. They do a fair trade in cigarettes too, splitting custom with 'Hiron's'. Although this aspect of their business is diminishing, it's still a corner of the market to which Dee would like exclusivity. She bemoans the competition.

I refrain from pointing out that 'Hiron's' has been on Southmead Road far longer than she.

＊

One area where Dee has a monopoly is alcohol sales. The nearest supermarket isn't that far away, and booze is cheaper there; even so, 'Six 'til Eight' has its loyal customers.

Like 'the great unwashed'. When he's in (his usual purchase is four cans of cheap cider, unless he's landed a touch in 'Willie's') there's nowhere to escape. I can't fabricate an excuse to go anywhere or talk to anyone, and often he's up at the till before I realise it, before I can make good my escape.

The first time people saw me there — those buying alcohol and who I knew from elsewhere — they instinctively became a little furtive, almost shy. One or two would pretend the gin or rum wasn't for them: "it's for our Jean". Over time most have become more cavalier, even to the extent of asking me if I've tried Ghostship or what I think of Bombay versus Gordon's. I'm not sure Dee is particularly appreciative of this interaction; I think she just wants to process the transaction and take their money as quickly as possible.

~

in Gripper Rod's

Some days it feels like walking in a forest. Those three metre rolls towering over narrow walkways like giant sequoia. And the unmistakeable smell of the hessian, wool, rubber. And when it's quiet (which is most of the time) there is a stillness not unlike a forest, punctuated only by the occasional chatter from the loading bay out back, or the click of Rod's fingers on his keyboard, his business-like voice punching vowels down the telephone.

❋

It is interesting watching people when they leaf through the heavy sample books. The ritual is almost always the same: the man retrieves the volume and finds a suitable surface upon which to lay it, and then the woman lifts each square of carpet one at a time. Hers is an action punctuated by short sentences, sometime single words: "too green", "not with our sofas", "ugh".

Rod usually gives them time to try out at least two books before he saunters over and asks if he can help.

"One book and they're only browsing," he tells me. "If it looks like they will go onto a third then it's much more serious. Decisions are likely to be made…" He winks, making it clear which one of the couple will be making the decisions.

~

in Alan's Brazils

Most people seem to expect Alan to know all there is to know about nuts and nutrients, supplements and vitamins, as if he is a bona fide member of the medical profession rather than a retailer: "My friend swears by glucosamine for her joints. Which of these would be best to start on, dosage-wise — and will they interfere with my statins?"

"If all these worked," he said to me once, casting an eye over his empire, "then I'd still feel twenty-five and be able to do fifty press-ups before I came here in the morning."

Alan's nearly fifty, looks closer to sixty, and appears as if three press-ups would be the end of him. He tells me he's had offers from Holland & Barrett regularly over the years, and though those offers might not be getting any larger they are looking more and more appealing.

＊

Almost every day I've been in there he's tried to sell me something based on an 'ailment' he's just spotted.

"You look a bit peaky; down on the Vitamin C?"

Occasionally the approach is more full-frontal.

"How are your movements — you know, 'down below'..? I've got a one-time deal on some mild and kind senna extract."

I'm not sure that's how you should talk to a potential customer, though maybe I should be flattered. Maybe he no longer sees me as a customer. Maybe he's just trying to help. 'Mild and kind' sums him up.

~

<u>in Hiron's</u>

When groups of kids come in on their way home from school you can see Ray shift to 'high alert'.

"They're more likely to pinch stuff on their way home," he said once. "Maybe they think they've got somewhere safe they can bolt to. If they try it on the way to school and get caught they know they'll be more likely to cop it."

He didn't indicate what the 'it' might be, merely nodding in my direction as if the secret was now shared.

"What you've got to watch out for is when one of them tries to grab your attention or hovers, taking too long to make their mind up. Mars or Snickers? Decoy tactics."

❊

Later.

"You know, when you've been sitting there working away the kids have been less likely to try something. As a rule I don't lose too much, but it's almost nothing when you're in. Extra pair of eyes and all that."

When he realised what he'd said I could see he was instantly worried I might want to take a cut.

"It's all pennies really."

❊

Rumour has it that Ray used to play professional football. I looked him up on the web and found a few old photos of someone who did and who shared his name; but I couldn't reconcile those images with the slightly bent sixty-four year old I knew.

I asked him once.

"Aye," he said, "a lot of people think that."

~

in Walter & Smyth (gents' outfitters)

I only see Walter very occasionally. He's too old and frail now to be much use in the shop, but he sometimes appears, perhaps for Old Times' sake.

I'd assumed 'Walter' and 'Smyth' would both be surnames, but before James Smyth became a partner the outfitter's had simply been known as 'Walter's'. The old man's surname being Higginbottom, they quickly ruled out 'Higginbottom and Smyth' as the establishment's revised name; "It wouldn't have created the right sort of impression," James once explained.

When he does appear, Walter is always immaculately dressed even now. I can imagine him in his pomp, preening about the place like a mannequin come to life; what better way to advertise your wares than by wearing them?

❋

Time passes more slowly here than in the other places. I daresay that's down to the scarcity of custom. If 'Six 'til Eight' is the commercial motorway of Southmead Road, then 'Walter and Smyth' is a single track road leading to a hamlet in Northumberland.

You get the picture.

❋

I want to ask James what their strategy is. With the other places it's fairly clear cut, driven either by purpose — the

Cancer shop and 'Daffodil's' — or commercial imperative i.e. turnover. More than anything else, 'Walter and Smyth' don't seem to want to be the arbiters of style but rather the guardians of tradition. Their jackets — all tweed and herringbone — went out of fashion thirty years ago; their casual wear is only casual if you are over fifty.

Is it ironic that I can spot things in the charity shops that were probably originally purchased here some years ago?

"We're just chugging along," James told me once. In consequence I propel myself forward thirty years and see *him* hobbling into view rather than Walter — and for nothing else to have changed.

He offers me a 'staff discount'. Although generous, I am not tempted.

~

in Eastman Estates

Several distinguishable types frequent Eastman's.

The Desperate. These are people who are either incredibly keen to sell their property or to buy one. They manifest their desperation via over-the-top enthusiasm and the frequency with which they cross the threshold. I wonder what drives the sellers? Surely more than a simple desire to leave the town; perhaps they have a pressing commitment elsewhere, like a new job. Or — if you wanted to be dramatic — perhaps they're running away from something, their attempt to escape driven by a modicum of fear. And the buyers? The opposites are clearly possible: the need to meet a deadline, or to make good their escape from somewhere else.

The Uncertain. I suppose these would be the equivalent of the 'browsers' in a conventional shop. They tend to be vague and non-committal when answering questions, filling in forms; they like to feel a substantial weight of physical property details in their hands, not merely to see what might be 'available' but perhaps those sheets of A4 have the power to help answer the key question which has been bothering them for far too long: "should we move?" Often 'the Uncertain' visit once and are never seen again, which — if my theory is correct — presumably indicates that they've finally made up their minds.

The Certain. These people know what they are about: they know what they are looking for, or are confident in what they are selling and why. They are business-like, decisive; there is nothing wishy-washy about them. Things are agreed, viewings arranged, deals are done, pragmatism wins out.

And for some people, Eastman's represents the backcloth for a journey: they start as Uncertain, become Certain, and then with the passage of time, potentially Desperate. It's a rite of passage for some — and difficult to watch.

§

"What do you think?"

Having taken my time in clearing the dinner things, I walk into the lounge to find the small sheaf of papers I had presented Cath now sitting in front of her on the coffee table. She is smiling — which is a start.

"You wrote this?" she asks playfully.

"No; I picked it up second-hand in the hospice shop!"

She laughs.

"So?" I worry my concern is too evident.

"What do you want me to say?" Then, before I can answer: "You know a writer's not supposed to ask family for any kind of critique?"

"Yes, because most family members can't be honest; you're putting them in an invidious position. I'm aware of all that. But you're not just any family. And neither was your mum."

"Meaning?"

"That you'll be honest. You can't not be."

I deliver it as an invitation: she can say what she likes. It's also a statement of trust — and that I need her to tell me the truth.

"It's so unlike anything you've ever written; if you hadn't told me, I wouldn't have believed it was yours."

"And is that good or bad? Because it could be the latter, obviously."

"Firstly, surprising. And secondly, good. I need to read it again — and I need to read more of it. But I'm there; I'm in those shops down the road; I can smell them, especially the mustiness of the charity shops."

"And 'the great unwashed'."

Again she laughs. "Is he for real?"

"As real as you and I — just not as clean."

I wait. It is a signal that I want more from her; that I need more. This isn't just about the writing per se, the ability to put one word in front of another. The question I need answering is whether I can successfully depict the real world — what I 'see' — as well as what I imagine I see. Or nearly as well. It's about exploding a myth. The fact that she thinks she can smell the Cancer shop and 'Daffodil's' is promising.

"And the style?" I can't avoid giving her a prompt.

"There are lot's of things it's not."

"Such as?"

"Oh, I don't know: romantic, fantastical, whimsical. Your normal stories are so lyrical in a way; they draw you in, pull you along."

My heart sinks. "And this doesn't?"

"Oh it does!" She delivers the phrase as if she feels she has committed some kind of faux pas. "But it's so 'real', so well-observed. And it's insightful too. Not that you don't see inside your fictional characters, you do; but here… These are real people. The odd remark, the odd phrase." She picks up the papers and flicks through them. "Like this: 'When he realised what he'd said I could see he was instantly worried I might want to take a cut.' And here: 'Alan's nearly fifty, looks closer to sixty, and appears as if three press-ups would be the end of him.' Or this: 'I'm not sure Dee is particularly appreciative of this interaction.' These are the skins of real people you've managed to get under."

"By seeing?" I suggest.

She smiles. "I know what you want me to say."

"Which is?"

"That you've proven you're able to 'see things'; which means your protestations that you couldn't have been false all these years. And it also proves that mum was right."

Now it is my turn to smile. "Of course she was. When wasn't she?"

The Piano Player

"I think," he said, his voice thickened by the resonance of a juvenile baritone which would only mellow over time, "I'm going to learn to play the piano."

His words were delivered with the degree of certainty which — although I missed it at the time — was to become his trademark as he grew older. In subsequent years, when it came to increasingly public pronouncements, you could never quite escape the sense of him weighing his words in advance, as if he had the capability to pre-process and rehearse them, to project their likely consequences before committing them to history. A long pause was usually the signal that something of relevance was coming. His delivery was his magic trick, his USP. Had he paused in such a fashion before stating his musical intention back when we were in our early twenties? I cannot recall. Nor can I recall the very last thing he said to me another thirty years further on — though I am certain it wasn't about the piano. How could it have been?

But I'm lying of course. I do remember the last thing he said to me, as I'm sure do all the other people who heard it.

The stated desire to play the piano suggested nothing more than a notion to try something new with which to fill his time. His was a diary which would only grow to bursting much later once his voice had been 'discovered' and when — after a television producer heard him read an audiobook and invited him for a screen test — it dawned on them that he was incredibly photogenic. The camera loved him. Back then all of that was in the future, and he had made his announcement sitting in a coffee outlet on the High Street, the pair of us killing time. It was as if he had calculated that spending some of his spare time on the piano would be appropriate. There was to be nothing frivolous. Even then he was nothing if not measured.

And throw himself at the piano he did. If he possessed one characteristic above all others it was to allow himself to become absorbed by something. It wasn't dedication, focus, or single-mindedness, but something more profound. Elemental even. Once he took on a 'thing' — whatever that 'thing' might be — it was as if he and it must become emotionally fused. When you see him now, striding across some ancient monument or strolling ever so slowly through an art gallery — all the while casually talking to the camera, to us — he has the uncanny ability to suggest he had been there when the monument wasn't ancient, or had been on-hand to clean Tintoretto's brushes as his masterpieces were being painted. His fans said he took 'authenticity' to a new level. They began to bracket him with Attenborough and Sharma, Beard and Cox. A few thought he excelled them. When pressed, he would demure, make comments about "the shoulders of giants".

If you asked Di what first captivated her (as I did on more than one occasion) she would confess it was his piano playing — and not because he was particularly fluent. "It had something to do with possession," she said to me once, "as if he and the piano were moulded into a single entity." You would have thought (I argued) that this might have ensured some degree of competence, if not brilliance, but it turned out that for all his sense of timing — seen to perfection later when delivering a line to a camera — he struggled with rhythm. "Rhythm with words is one thing," she said, "but with music it's something else entirely."

And she should have known. Already heading towards her own kind of stardom, Di became his informal tutor as he strived to climb proficiency's ladder. That she should fall in love with him along the way was hardly surprising — in the same way that it was unsurprising he would give up on the piano as soon as it became clear that Grade 4 was his limit. Realising Di was going to make her living as a concert pianist didn't help either. He couldn't bear to live in anyone's shadow.

Back then I was merely an adjunct, a hanger-on. I was his 'best mate'. We were still young enough for such appellations to be credible. When it came to Di, I was something of a counsellor too, helping him navigate the foothills of their relationship, the minor partner in our trio until he didn't need me any more. Occasionally we'd make up a foursome, often at his insistence and usually with someone Di knew; but after three months or so my services were no longer needed and I left them to it. I still saw him from time-to-time of course; that was how he kept me abreast of his struggles with the piano — and Di's complete mastery of the same instrument. I asked him if it was irksome that he was in love with someone who was better at something than he was. The way he looked at me suggested such a question did not compute.

Our face-to-face interactions incrementally reduced, I came to see more of him on television than I did in real life. It was impossible not to marvel at how he managed to blend authority with that relaxed way he had; how he wrapped up his viewers and listeners with that voice of his. I used to wait for his tell-tale pauses and think "here it comes!" And Di? She was rarely on television at all. Indeed, I can only recall one appearance at the Proms a few years after I met her. But she was keen on social media, and kept people updated as to what she was doing — and sometimes what *they* were doing. Together they made quite a couple, and when the media became interested in them it was, of course, largely thanks to his popularity. There were two Radio Times pieces: one for a new documentary series of his, and one for the pair of them triggered by Di's Proms outing. When they moved to the country, a magazine persuaded them to let a reporter-cum-photographer rove the house and gardens asking questions and taking photos.

I don't know for sure, but that might have marked the beginning of the turning of things. Although she liked to be present on Social Media, Di was essentially a private person; he, on the other hand, came to enjoy the limelight, the recognition. Notoriety was — he once argued — useful as a hook to get people engaged; once they were engaged, that was what gave him the chance to inform and educate. Whether justification or window-dressing, it was a theory I'm sure he believed.

The events which truly undermined them began when Di landed an extended tour of Europe where she had been engaged to play fourteen concerts. Her time away only partially overlapped the two months he was due to spend in Antarctica putting together a short series on isolation and the effect extreme environments have on people. Di returned from Europe three days after he had flown south.

Was it ironic that one of the effects of his isolation from her was to expose how weak the foundations of their relationship had become? He had not seemed to suffer at all while she had been on tour — at least not as far as I could see. Indeed, one of the 'red tops' ran a story suggesting that, thanks to a somewhat younger BBC researcher, he had found an interim substitute for her. I doubted the story, and when I challenged him, he denied it. I couldn't believe he was made that way. I didn't think any of us were. The story reached Di of course, and out of the blue she rang me from Stuttgart one evening to ask me if I thought it was true. I tried to be as categorical in my denial as I could be, replaying to her what he had told me. But the seed had been sown. It was only later we found out that the same researcher had been assigned to the Antarctic project — though, of course, that didn't of itself prove anything.

Yet it was Di who went off-the-rails first. Returning home to an empty house and exhausted from her tour, initially she revelled in the peace and quiet, the being alone. And then, thinking about him thousands of miles away at the foot of the world — and on the back of those rumours — she found herself asking what she missed most about him. Unable to answer the question to her satisfaction, she binge-watched his two most recent tv series looking for clues. What she saw, she told me, was the personality not the man; she saw the product he had become, not the man she had fallen in love with. No matter how hard she tried, she simply couldn't find that person in the image on the screen. Invited to stay for a weekend soon after to the onset of this strange period, at one point I walked into the living room to find him in freeze-frame on their over-sized television with Di sitting about three feet away. She looked like a detective searching for clues.

I had always liked her, of course; it was impossible not to. She had a charm and elegance about her; she was genuine, soft and warm. And she had the most marvellous hands. Oh I know it's hardly original to make such a comment about a pianist — it might even be considered trite — but her fingers were so slender, her skin pale and unblemished. I swear she could have played Rachmaninov on a potato peeler! When, half way through his Antarctic project, the 'Love in a Cold Climate' article about him and the researcher was published, she beckoned me again to their house. Should I have been surprised that she sought me out for more than simple emotional support? You might argue that I should have been honourable and thought of my friend, but Di was my friend too. I'm not going to say that I took pity on her or was seeking some kind of victory over him, because neither of those are true — at least not in my eyes.

Not wanting to face a potentially ugly scene when he returned a month later — in her mind a scene arising from what he, not she, had done — she chose to come and stay with me. "Just for a while," she said. It was a while which lasted five years.

Their unravelling had the blessing of being swift — and the curse of being played out in the public domain. Although he denied the stories about the BBC researcher, the young woman concerned had moved into his house within a few weeks. I couldn't help but wonder whether Di's pre-emptive strike had actually brought him and the researcher together. After a short while cause and effect didn't seem to matter. His Antarctic series was a great hit, and as a result America came calling.

He lives in California still, basking in a slightly modified, more 'Hollywood' kind of celebrity. And Di? She played fewer concerts it's true — and never again out of the UK — but was always lauded wherever she performed. The contract with Deutsche Grammophon landed in her lap six months before she was diagnosed, and she managed to fulfil a third of her recording obligations before she had to renege on the deal. Her final recording — of Gershwin's *Rhapsody in Blue* — is widely regarded as one of the finest interpretations ever. I find I can no longer listen to it.

It was nearly a year after Di's death I bumped into him again. He was back in the UK to promote a series on deserts he had put together for Netflix. We just happened to be in the same West End restaurant, he arriving with his entourage just as I was leaving with my publisher. The years — and probably the desert — had taken their toll, but it was evident he now had a ruggedness to go with the voice, that authority.

We both stopped when we caught sight of each other. There was no recognition other than a stare, no movement toward a handshake, no attempt at a smile — just that tell-tale pause.

"You bastard. You took her from me."

And then the encounter was over. For a moment I thought he might have tried to lay me out.

So those were his words; words that were repeated in several newspaper articles the following day. In the restaurant they had been accompanied by the flash from a few phone cameras, the outputs from which were similarly broadcast. It was, I suppose, to be my own five minutes of fame.

just a skein of wool

then someone said it didn't matter if what i believed in or did wasn't actually real and i thought what's that supposed to mean it doesn't matter and just as i was trying to parse that and my apparent unimportance then the second part of what they said hit me the part about it not being real at all presumably their underlying point something to do with the nature of reality and what that is etcetera on that basis how can you know if anything is real though i guess if you don't think you know what real is or can't define it adequately never mind see or touch it then nothing's going to matter to you is it i mean how can it

i met someone once who thought people weren't real and were just bits and bytes of computer code that had been dropped into a kind of virtual reality world to see how we functioned as if we were lab rats highly sophisticated lab rats in a keanu reeves' matrix-type environment with one all-powerful being sitting at a cosmic keyboard somewhere punching in numbers and instructions and taking decisions for us and all the while we were deluding ourselves in thinking that we were making the choices and so if that bonkers notion was true then think of all the lies we would have been fed over the years never mind free will or that nothing we saw or felt was an actual thing etcetera all of which made me think the person who'd said that thing about us being virtual was just a nut-job swallowing all that shit about us being non-entities running around inside some great computer not that i knew that particular idiot well enough to pass judgement actually not well at all in fact or maybe it's just that our bytes haven't collided yet or something but i do know the person who thought what i said and did didn't matter because i've known them for as long as i can remember and usually they've been a decent enough person someone i could rely on for advice even if it was hardly impartial even if it was downright biased but that's what friends are for isn't it though having said that what they're not for is to tell you that all the stuff that's important to you might not matter to them or anyone else or might not be real whatever the hell they meant by that and even if i don't know i suspect they might not know either so maybe that's what i should do press them on their statement ask for justification or reasoning and probe the theories behind what may or may not have been their underlying premise if they had one or then again maybe they were just shooting the breeze coming up with whatever popped into their head at that precise moment like most of us do i suppose and most of the time too unless big brother is tapping away at his or her keyboard like some kind of dervish sending us left or right up or down

not that i believe that computer stuff to be true but wouldn't it be scary if it was all the while undermining those things you've built your life around like family and friendships and love and belief systems all of them swept away blown away like you might blow dust from the surface of your glasses to allow you to see better and then how would you undo all that past stuff not undo it in the sense of turning back time and making it not happen because life's not like doctor who but in terms of what it and they did to you or how they or it made you feel and shape what you did next and then everything after that too and it would be like taking the biggest jumper in the world and starting to unpick it unravelling the wool and watching the pile grow at your feet until you were holding nothing in your hands and all you had was this tangle of yarn that didn't mean anything that didn't matter and that might in the end prove to be more real that the jumper you'd been holding in the first place

think about that and think about what that would do to you and how much you'd be fucked up to suddenly realise that what you thought was a thing wasn't one any longer and that reality was just a mess like a big pile of wool shapeless at your feet

The Contract

It's important to make it clear from the outset that I am not an advocate of arranged marriages. In terms of my own future, an arranged marriage was not something I had ever countenanced, considered or entertained. Indeed, they are so far from the norm in our culture — one which, for as long as anyone can remember, regards an individual's choice as sacrosanct — that they are the rarest of outliers. Almost mythological. That is until there is a greater imperative, a higher calling if you will. It was in such a way that the notion was first suggested to me, couched in hypothetical terms. Then, having been broached, the hypothetical quickly turned to suggestion, the suggestion to vague proposal. Soon — maybe in the very same conversation with my father, I don't recall — the vague morphed into the concrete. And before I knew it, the concrete had a name. Zahra.

Perhaps I should explain.

No-one can recall how it started. It was so long ago that those who were around at the time have long since died. At one point (the story goes) someone insulted someone else. Our tribe or theirs, it hardly matters. Indeed there may not have been such recognisable entities at the time; perhaps they arose later, collections of people gradually fused together through a commonality of goal or belief. In any event, that first insult was returned and — as is the way in such matters — delivered with a little 'interest'. Feeling the response unjustified, the first party now believed *they* had been wronged and had the right of redress. And so the cycle began. Insignificant at first, the scale of increment on each response was almost negligible. Almost. Years passed. Decades even. People pretend they can put a date on the first trespass, the first robbery, the first time violence of any significance was used. Perhaps that is so. But the first death is known, certain; a fixed point on the journey of both our cultures. As is sadly the norm, inevitably one death became two, two became three, and so on. There was an escalation in weaponry, and a reduction in the consideration as to how those weapons were used. Collateral damage rose in our collective social conscience not only as an every-day term, but as an evil to be lived with — because it was considered better than the alternative of shame, capitulation, defeat.

What began as a slow crawl toward the abyss had — seemingly in the blink of an eye — turned into a gallop.

Then two wise men were brave enough to attempt to divest themselves of generations of bias, and took the trouble to look openly at the on-rushing horizon. One was my father, a senior member of our ruling council; the other, his opposite number. And because they considered their shared and damned future to be all too-short, they dared to talk. How might they stop the downward spiral into chaos, that was the question.

Choosing to talk when it was our 'turn' to retaliate allowed my father to occupy the moral high ground (if there could ever be such a thing in circumstances like ours). What, he asked, would it take to stop the senseless pursuit of mutual destruction? The two men began to use words like 'link' and 'bridge', discussed concepts such as 'mutuality' and 'common interest'. Carried out in secret, no-one was aware of the timespan of the debates, only that one day the two men took their joint proposal to our respective ruling councils. It would, my father told them, require a sacrifice on each side. And then he offered me. His counterpart offered his daughter. In many ways it was a return to compromise from a simpler time.

When in principle the deal was struck there was no immediate fanfare. In order to prevent an exaggeration of hope — or a wave of hysteria or backlash — the proposal was closely guarded; before going public they needed the agreement of the two key players, namely myself and Zahra. We believed Zahra would not be an issue given what we knew of our adversary's culture: she would be told, and that would be the end of it. In my case, my father was adamant that it should be my choice; I needed to agree, he would not force me to do anything. Yet how could I say no? Given what the union would represent — the opportunity to replace a doomed future with a brighter and more optimistic one — how could I do other than acquiesce?

All of which resulted in my parents, a few dignitaries, and myself, standing in a small temporary tented structure located precisely on the border between our two lands. We were impatiently awaiting the arrival of my bride. She was late — but then wasn't that the bride's prerogative?

Four women and one man entered the tent. I took the man and the eldest of the women to be my father's counterpart and his wife. The men shared the briefest of nods. Where on our side we had taken the trouble to dress smartly (suits and such like), the three younger women who had just entered were casually attired: jeans, white t-shirts, trainers. At least they all matched! During those first few tension-filled moments, the female newcomers acknowledged no-one but each other, talking in an animated way in a language I struggled to place. Then one of them — the tallest of the three — made her way towards me. Still without any eye-contact, she turned on her heel immediately in front of me and then took a step backwards. My reaction — to put out my hands and place them on her waist to prevent her crashing into me — was an instinctive one and, from the way she then settled, entirely expected.

An awkward hush descended. Having this young woman slightly swaying mere centimetres from me, the two of us joined by my hands on her hips, seemed the strangest of introductions. I glanced at my father to see if he could rescue me from my unusual predicament, but he remained resolutely stoney-faced. Then I became aware that everyone's eyes — except for the one person whose eyes I wanted to see most of all — were fixed on me. Clearly it was supposed to be my turn.

"Shall I be the first to make the introductions?"

On hearing my voice, the young woman released my hold by taking several resolute steps away from me, then turned to face the entrance. Her two companions followed suit, and this seemed a trigger for the rest of us to do likewise.

At that moment a fourth young woman entered the tent. A metre in, she paused, nodded to the older couple, then to my father and mother; then she turned to face me. Although slightly shorter than her similarly dressed friends, Zahra was endowed with the same long black hair and slightly narrow face that was a common characteristic of women of her tribe. Also wearing jeans and a white t-shirt, she had chosen to accessorise them with a gold necklace and matching earrings; on both wrists she wore gold bangles which — when she started walking towards me — jangled slightly thanks to her loose stride. She stopped immediately in front of me and said my name. "Zahra" I responded. There was a slight smile on her lips as she glanced down to where my hands hung limply at my side, then, raising one in her own, said "Please introduce me to your family".

From that moment, the tension which had been building simply evaporated. I introduced her to my parents, she to hers. The young woman who had planted herself so forcefully in front of me proved to be her sister. It had been, she told me later, "a kind of test" — though of what I remained ignorant. After a short while there was a ceremony presided over by our parents (the formal wedding pageant would come later), and then we were escorted to another pavilion where food had been prepared. It was with a mix of relief and pride I noted both our sets of parents sitting together, the two men — in spite of all the history between them — relaxed in each other's company. And throughout all of this, Zahra did not let go of my hand.

"You are aware of the conditions attached to our coming together?" she asked at one point, her voice lowered to a whisper. Even at that early stage hers was a voice I found intoxicating.

"About the children?"

She nodded. "The first two, one given over to each family to look after, to nurture."

"Part of the bonds to keep us joined."

There was a pause.

"In our family there is a tradition of twins in the female line," she said. Then another pause. "After that, the rest of the children are for us." She squeezed my hand, and then turned to talk to her sister.

For the next hour there was food and drink, then some music and a little dancing. By early evening it was as if we had all known each other for years, as if there had never been an insult in the first place.

A little before ten, Zahra took me by the arm and drew me to one side and out into the night.

"So it begins," she said.

Unreliable Witness

"What was your name again?"

He was being led away from the Public Conveniences when he accosted me. Okay it was only a very mild verbal assault, but he had a manner about him — slightly wild and edgy — which suggested, even in that brief moment, that had he not been accompanied the verbal might have quickly turned to something else.

"Come on, Simmo," his minder said, casting me an apologetic look, his raised eyebrows adding the silent accompaniment: "what's he like?" or "what am I supposed to do with him?"

Before we go any further I should make it plain that I had never seen 'Simmo' before. Nor his minder. Yet it was all too easy to typecast the former based on his appearance, and, as such, someone who in the normal course of events would not be too difficult to forget. In addition to his vaguely 'unhinged' demeanour, he was sporting about two weeks' worth of unremarkable beard and was wearing cheap-looking black tracksuit-bottoms above somewhat grubby white Nike trainers. Waist-up he sported a replica football shirt of some tribe or other which was partially obscured by an unzipped dark blue fleece. Although early summer, it was clearly something to be worn at Yuletide. The two words emblazoned across its front were split in half by the zip; in consequence, the right-hand side displayed 'Fat Chris', the left 'her tmas'. For an instant I wondered what a 'tmas' might be, and why it should be 'hers'.

All in all its owner had the air of a man without any possessions of note, nor the means to acquire them. Based on that brief coming together, I decided he wouldn't have known what to do with money had he any — apart from the obvious (typecasting again!): cigarettes, or cans of Tennant's 'Super' or whatever the modern-day equivalent was. Assuming he might occasionally be permitted unaccompanied excursions, perhaps he might indulge in something illegal scored off a bloke he knew at 'The Navigation'. No-one with any sense drank in 'The Navigation'.

In spite of my being able to categorise Simmo in this somewhat lazy way — and instinctively believing I could file him away in my mental rubbish bin — when I left the toilets a few minutes later I found myself still shaken by the encounter. (I nearly said 'ordeal', but it was hardly that.) Had I previously met Simmo and simply forgotten him? Was he someone I'd known in my past life now changed beyond recognition? Or was it possible that his chaperone had triggered the encounter by whispering something in his ear akin to "there's that chap I was telling you about"?

I ruled all three out. It was just a random coming together, the result of a roll of life's dice.

§

Whoever was rolling those dice did so again a few days later.

There was something in the air and the colour of the sky to suggest we were due our first real taste of summer. Spring had been a little bit hit-and-miss: hot spell, then cold snap; cold snap, then hot spell. But the combination that day — clouds of a different shape and fewer of them, almost no breeze — felt a little like finally bringing the curtain down on an impetuous season.

I had taken the opportunity for a long lunch and walked from the office into the local park. Buying a coffee and a slice of Rocky Road from its café, I settled on one of the benches to watch a game of bowls which — hearing the scores shouted out at each end — had clearly been going on for some time. Having finished my snack, I turned to throw the detritus into a nearby bin when, in doing so, I saw Simmo enter the park. Choosing to walk away from the bowling green, he shuffled more than walked towards the empty bandstand. Having had that one brief encounter with him, I admit I was somewhat fascinated. Head down, the hood of his 'Fat Chris' fleece over his head, he moved like a man who was striving to keep a secret to himself, as if any sign of openness, any unnecessary gesture, might betray him.

When he reached the bandstand he walked up its steps and then, positioning himself in its centre, sat down cross-legged. Unable to suppress them, I found myself wrestling with questions once again. Where was his minder? Was he waiting for someone — and if so, who? I also wondered what he might have been up to since our lavatorial encounter. I had been to work, done my weekly shop, gone to watch football at the weekend, thought about phoning my parents, missed my ex-girlfriend. There wasn't much in that list that was out of the ordinary, and — if you don't include the result of the football match — only one thing that was painful. But Simmo? What did 'normal' look like for him?

"Thirteen-twelve," came a call from the bowls match. "Our end."

I checked my watch. I had about fifteen minutes before I needed to be getting back; there was a team meeting at two which would inevitably go on for far too long and, in consequence, leave me an hour or so to try and resolve an issue in the program I had been debugging for days. My boss wanted an update at five and I had little in the way of good news for her. My software was on her 'critical path', something she never tired of telling me.

The next end in the game was a tense one resulting in the two nearest bowls needing their distance from the jack to be measured. When a score of thirteen-all was announced I found myself wishing I could get another coffee and spend the rest of the afternoon seeing how the match played out; it would certainly have been preferable to the team meeting. However, given that was not an option, I rose and stretched. As I did so I looked over and saw the bandstand was now unoccupied.

"I *do* know you," said a voice to my right.

I knew who it was before I turned my head.

Simmo was smaller than I'd remembered him from our previous coming together, though the rest of his weasel-like appearance was the same. There was a nasal quality in his voice and he spoke from a stooped position, his head slightly to one side, as if it had become his habit to be ingratiating and obsequious. For an instant he looked like a character from Dickens.

"Sorry," I said, adopting the default tone of voice I reserved to dismiss buskers, charity workers, street beggars, and sellers of *The Big Issue*.

"From outside the gents," he persisted.

"I need to be getting back to work."

It sounded like an excuse, but I assumed it would be enough to see him off. Beginning to walk away, I was confident of being able to quickly put some distance between us.

"The Council. Yeah, I know."

His statement was enough to cause me to pause and turn his way. In that instant he had shuffled beside me.

"How do you know where I work?"

"Because of Big Mick."

"'Big Mick'?"

"The guy you saw me with that day."

"I thought he was…" I began in spite of myself, then was immediately unwilling to tell him what I'd actually thought.

"Yeah, he was looking after me." Simmo continued walking forward and I found myself in-step beside him. "I'd had a bad day. Or a bad night before. You know." He waited for an acknowledgement which I refrained from giving. "Anyway, I wanted to apologise."

"Apologise?"

"For before. Coming across all… I don't know. I was still a bit wired I suppose."

I nodded, assuming his confession would mark the end of our dialogue; but then I realised there was a loose end that needed tying. I hate loose ends — which was one of the reasons not being able to fix my program was nagging at me so much.

"How does 'Big Mick' know where I work?"

Simmo laughed, as if I'd missed the most obvious connection in the world.

"Because of Miss Watson."

"Miss Watson?"

"The lady what you works for. She helps out at the hostel sometimes. Knows Big Mick. Pointed you out to him one weekend when you was shopping in town. Something like that."

The connection floored me. Juliet — 'Miss Watson' — was as hard-nosed a boss as I'd ever worked for; she was driven by results, and results at all costs. I'd never seen an ounce of compassion in her. And now here was this urchin, telling me something about her I didn't know.

"Small world," I offered, trying to hide the fact that I was now slightly off-balance; bemused that she deemed me significant enough to be pointed out to 'Big Mick'.

"Ain't it just?"

§

Having been briefly detained in the park by Simmo, I only just made it back to the office in time for the meeting and was last to take my seat. This was out of the ordinary for two reasons: first, because I'm habitually early for everything so never rush anywhere; and second, because I always sit in the same place. That afternoon I hurried through the door and had to take the only seat left. Juliet raised an eyebrow at my out-of-character entrance. "If we're all ready," she said.

Once she started speaking — her opening, the usual state-of-the-project address — I found myself paying extra attention, trying to reconcile my new knowledge of her against months and months of practical experience. The Juliet who focussed on numbers and trends, dates and deadlines, seemed too far removed from an individual who was compelled to give up their free time to help out at a homeless charity. It was this blend — the dullness of the team meeting alongside newly acquired intrigue — which saw me endure the session in an entirely new way.

At the end Juliet asked me to stay back.

"Is there anything wrong?" she asked.

144

"Wrong?" I assumed it was a genuine question, and a work-related one. I slipped back in 'programmer mode' and became a coder needing to try and solve an unrelenting conundrum.

"You were late in — which isn't an issue of course, but so unlike you. And then your update was" — she paused — "brief."

"I didn't think there was much to say." Straight bat, work-wise.

"But throughout you seemed distracted somehow. Is there anything the matter?"

She was nothing if not perceptive, I'll give her that. And there seemed just a trace of concern in her voice. Just a few hours earlier I would have put such an anomaly down to nothing more than naïve misinterpretation on my part.

"I've just had some news," I said, letting my guard down — then instantly regretted that I'd done so.

"Nothing serious, I hope."

It was clear that she had instantly assumed my 'news' was grave, that it involved ill health, either mine or someone in my family. Or even a death. There was no way I could allow her to think that. I may be many things, but I like to think I'm reasonably honest.

"Not 'news' exactly." I hesitated. "More like information."

The word sounded clumsy on my lips and must have made its way into the world in a kind of semi-strangled way because Juliet raised an eyebrow.

Now I had a binary choice: lie or tell the truth.

"I've just met an acquaintance of yours."

Ten minutes later we were sitting in her office drinking coffee.

"I knew my involvement with Paddock House would become public knowledge at some point," she said. We were across from each other at her small meeting table. "I hoped I might remain incognito for just a little longer."

"I wouldn't say it was public knowledge." I tried to sound reassuring. "It's only me, and I've told no-one."

"And will you?"

For the first time — perhaps ever — it felt as if we were embarking on a discussion as equals.

"I hadn't planned on doing so. None of my business really. And if you'd rather I didn't, then I won't."

"Thanks. I'd appreciate that."

There was an obvious question.

"But why don't you want anyone to know? I mean, it's not as if you're an axe murderer or anything."

She laughed — which was a first. Strange how you can instantly change your perception of someone thanks to something as innocent as a laugh.

"I just want to keep work and play separate. There's no overlap. And the goals and drivers are completely different. I treat them as disconnected, playing to different parts of me. I suppose that was what I was aiming to achieve. I don't want people thinking I'm soft."

I laughed, because I was supposed too. I also managed *not* to say "no chance of that!"

"Who told you?" she asked.

"I think his name is Simmo."

"Simpson?" Her brow furrowed with instant recognition. "I've told him nothing. Wouldn't dream of it."

"Then 'Big Mick' might be the culprit," I suggested.

She took a sip of her coffee. I could see her attempting to join dots: what she'd said to whom; who might have said what to someone else. I suppose I could have tried to help clarify — assuming Simmo was telling the truth — but chose not to.

"Well."

And she drew a line under the conversation.

§

Of course none of that actually happened. A plausible fantasy, you might say.

It might have been nice if we *had* sat in Juliet's office and she divulged some tragedy in her childhood — parents dying too young perhaps — which now, as an adult, incentivised her to help others who, largely through no fault of their own, found themselves in a similar situation.

Which was Simmo's story, more or less, divulged to me as we sat in the park.

His view of 'Ms Watson' was verging on the agricultural, but believable none the less. She had been introduced to help mentor a therapy group in which he occasionally participated "when I've nothing better to do, or they make me." She was an immediate hit, not because of what she did or what she said, but because she had slim ankles.

"Lovely legs," Simmo slithered. "Have you ever noticed? 'Specially when she's wearing high heels. That's what we noticed first. Took our minds off the boring chit-chat. Gave us something to fantasise about; know what I mean?"

When he started to tell me what some of the other men in the group said they would like to do with their new helper I told him that I'd got the picture. I can't say I'd noticed Juliet's legs particularly, but then I don't suppose I'm what you'd call 'a leg man'.

Seeing I wasn't going to be drawn into anything lascivious, he told me that Ms Watson most often came into Paddock House on Saturday mornings, helped out in the kitchen when she wasn't running some sort of discussion group. "When I know she's going to be in I try to make myself available." He sniggered at the inappropriate phrase. "Often Big Mick is in those groups, sitting at the back. He's her chaperone I suppose. First he'd tries to make sure as many attend as possible, and then sits there keeping an eye on us. Legs or no legs, it's always boring."

The question as to why he was associated with the place begged to be asked. He laughed when I suggested he lived there.

"Me? I'm what you call a 'casual guest'. I drop in from time-to-time. Sometimes voluntarily, sometimes not. Depends. If I've had a bad night it might be the old Bill finds me somewhere I shouldn't be; or Big Mick comes across me when he goes on one of his late night walks. 'Patrols' he calls them. They'd never let Ms Watson go on one of those 'patrols'…" He cackled again.

I confess that at this point I'd lost all sense of time. We'd sat down on a bench near the entrance (or Simmo had chosen to sit down and I'd found myself compelled to sit alongside him) then he'd lured me in like a champion angler.

"Me?" He paused for effect when I pushed him for his story. "A tragic case, your lordship. Father ran off when I was a baby; mother got in with the wrong sort and ended up on the game, doing drugs. What chance did I have? She had me fetching and carrying for her when I was thirteen. Know what I mean? Ended up paying me in kind." Another laugh. "Petty crime and drugs. A police record. I was weak-willed. Or trapped. Not like your lordship. Or Ms Watson. Paddock's my safety net. But at least I know that and can see it for what it is — both the place and my life. There are some little shits who…" He stopped himself. "'Ere, shouldn't you be getting back to work?"

I checked my watch. I was going to be late.

"Before you go, spare a few bob for a cuppa?"

And I was late. Juliet had already started the meeting when I entered the conference room.

Like most people there, I went through the next couple of hours on autopilot. I'd hoped to be able to validate Simmo's assessment about Juliet's ankles but she was wearing a trouser suit and, no matter how she stood or sat, there was no way I could conjure an appropriate viewing angle.

At the end of the meeting she asked me to stay back.

"I'm worried," she said. "You were late today, which isn't like you. On its own that's nothing really, but you've been struggling to resolve this coding issue — which also isn't like you — and I can't help but get the sense that there's an underlying problem. Is there something going on I should know about?"

I could tell you that at this point I dropped the Simmo bombshell in her lap and that, as a result, we went into her office and drank coffee and chatted like two normal civilised human beings — but then I've already tried that one.

Or that I didn't mention Paddock House at all, but mumbled some excuse about the program and assured her I'd have it sorted by the end of the week.

Or that she fired me there and then, and in order to get my own back I told everyone about her charitable moonlighting — and her ankles — as I made my way out of the office.

Or confess that none of that's true either.

If you must know, I'd told Simmo to fuck off. I felt threatened okay, and I don't respond well to pressure — especially when it's applied in a public setting. I may even have shoved him a little.

I almost ran out of the park.

Once back at work I immediately went to wash my hands as if doing so would remove all trace of him. Then I got my stuff together and went to the meeting. I was as prompt as usual, sat in my normal seat, gave my usual update. It was boring yes, but I got through it. There was no staring at Juliet's ankles, no daydreaming about her role at Paddock House or what motivated her to volunteer there. She didn't call me back at the end of the session. And we didn't have coffee together.

When I got back to my desk I switched on my computer and got back to work. Oddly, I found the bug in my program almost instantly; a misplaced keystroke, that's all it was. I ran a few tests, confirmed it was working, then went to tell Juliet. "Well done," was all she said.

It was enough for me to allow myself to wind down for the day. One last cup of coffee, a few emails. I knew what was next on my work list and decided I'd start on that in the morning.

I'm quite lucky where I sit in the office in that I've a window seat; they're like gold dust! It's probably because I've been there a while longer than most other members of the team. Or maybe it was chance, a roll of the dice. Anyway, the window overlooks the main entrance of the building and down towards the front gates and the main road. I often look out of the window as I'm putting my coat on at the end of the day. Just habit I suppose. That day when I did so, I saw a slightly stooped and shabbily-dressed figure just outside the gates, the hood on his fleece pulled over his head. He was waiting — and there could only be two people for whom he was on the lookout.

Or then again, maybe he wasn't there at all…

Rescue

She is watching Amber die and expecting a miracle. When they asked her if she wanted to stay for the final moments, what could she do other than say 'yes'? Years before she had seen *Ghost* and fallen in love; not with Patrick Swayze (nor Demi Moore, come to that!) but with the idea of the soul leaving the body at its end, living on forever in the ether. It had become *her* film — and a kind of informal religion too. Although she had never investigated the subject in any meaningful way (she wasn't religious, after all) she believed there were some faiths — Eastern, she assumed — where it was readily accepted that the soul was a discrete entity in its own right. What's more, it was immortal. If that were the case, then why shouldn't it be possible for other creatures to have souls too? It was a theory — Buddhist or otherwise — that suited her.

They had brought Amber into the vet's some half-an-hour previously. There had been no crisis, no accident, just the penultimate scene in the theatre of her decline — failing eyesight, decreasing mobility. The ageing she had been fighting against for so long was finally going to overwhelm her. Leaving Ben in a waiting area awash with animals whose owners appeared more sick than they, she had accompanied Amber into the examination room. As soon as the vet uttered the word 'kindness' she knew what it meant; it was one of those shorthand words, a coded message. She had listened, stroked Amber's head. And now, the coup de grace administered, she is waiting for the moment of release. Not that she expects to see Amber's soul leave her body — if it were that obvious there would be no mystery or miracle! — but rather she expects to have a sense of it, that ultimate moment. She thinks she will *know*. Strangely, in spite of former instructions, she wonders if she shouldn't have had Ben in there with her — even if he would have gone to pieces and she end up distracted, needing to keep him upright, under control, and therefore miss the instant when Amber is finally freed.

But irrespective of Ben's presence or absence, miss it she does. There is no hiatus or climactic moment. She sees and feels nothing.

"There." The vet's voice intrudes on any potential reverie, his single word delivered like a full stop. "Would you like to keep her collar and name tag?"

She looks at the dead animal on the table and finds it almost unrecognisable. If that was as close as she would come to a moment of release, it is entirely inappropriate. A betrayal.

"No. Thank you."

"You've done the right thing," the vet offers, a practiced hand on her arm for a moment. "Please see the desk on the way out."

Payment. Another coded message, like "kindness" and "there". She nods. Ben will handle that; he's better with money.

§

"How was it?"

There are in the car. Ben has turned the key in the ignition but they have yet to move. On appearing empty-handed from the treatment room, Ruth had pointed him at the receptionist and left the building. When he too emerged she was standing by the car, waiting. His question is the first exchange between them for perhaps twenty minutes.

"Peaceful." Not that she knows what that really means. But it seems appropriate, what Ben might have expected to hear; perhaps it is even reassuring. In it's own way it's another word borrowed from a codebook built up over time, a lexicon shaped by experience and culture.

Had it been peaceful for Amber? Ruth has no idea. She probably wouldn't have felt the needle; perhaps she would merely have been overcome with tiredness. If there had been a soul released, it might have said "finally", or "thank you". But all that is guesswork. Given other potentially more traumatic endings, Ruth chooses to feel they have done the best they could. On that basis, 'peaceful' is as good as any other description.

Ben places a hand on her leg and gives it a gentle squeeze, then transfers it to the gear stick and begins to reverse out of the parking space.

§

Walking through the kitchen door the first thing Ruth sees is Amber's water bowl in the corner near the sink. She freezes. Strangely alert, Ben brushes wordlessly past her, picks it up, then goes with it into the utility room. Now it is his turn to reappear empty-handed.

Ruth is struck by the action, not merely how pragmatic and practical it is, but how it feels driven by a concern for her. Amber had essentially been 'Ben's dog': he had been first among equals; the one who took on the bulk of walking duties; the person at whose feet Amber preferred to lay when they were watching television. Ruth knows he might have crumbled at that instant — as much as he might have done in the vet's.

"Thanks," she says.

"I'll sort all that out in a bit." The vagueness is enough. "Do you want tea?"

Without waiting for a response, Ben lifts the kettle and moves to the sink to fill it. In doing so, Ruth notices his foot strays into the space where the dog's bowl had been; were it still there, Ben would have kicked water all over the floor. She wonders what that might mean; whether he has already 'moved on'. Or perhaps he is simply putting her first.

"Thanks," she says again.

§

In the lounge, Ruth sits in her chair reading the local paper. On the sofa, Ben flicks through last month's edition of *Amateur Photographer*. Glancing down at his feet, she sees Amber isn't there. It is still early enough to be a shock. She wonders about the gap that has suddenly appeared in their lives, the things they will no longer need to do or buy.

"Will you miss her?" Even though it is a question with only one possible answer, she feels compelled to ask it. Indeed all the newly opened-up spaces demand she does so. She glances at the clock. In thirty minutes Ben will not stand up, will not look down to Amber, will not ask if she wants to go for a walk, will not laugh at the remnants of the old dog's enthusiasm.

"Of course," he says. "But this day has been coming for long enough for us to be prepared. Don't you think?"

If his pragmatism and lack of emotion surprises her, it is no more surprising than the odd combination of shock and loss *she* currently feels. There is a question forming in her mind: take Amber away and what is left? Yes, just the two of them, obviously; the two of them with their cars and jobs, living their comfortable lives in their comfortable house. But now with something missing. And in trying to rationalise what that missing piece is — not Amber herself, but what she represented — Ruth reconstitutes the animal as a kind of glue, a conduit for connectivity, communication, common feeling, shared experience. What does it mean that Amber will no longer be there? And what external force will now keep them together? Certainly not the local paper and *Amateur Photographer*.

"Do you want to get another one?" Suddenly frightened by the potential of a gap between them, Ruth rushes out the question.

"A bit early to say," Ben looks across to her, "but I don't think so. I've been thinking about that too, and well, wouldn't it be nice not to have the tie — for a while at least, until things settle down? We could take that long holiday we've been putting off for years. Just as an example."

Although struck by how well he has prepared himself, how he is presenting a perfectly logical argument, Ruth is also aware of all those things he is not saying. Codewords again. Amber not being there offers them an opportunity for something else too, for the one thing Ben has most wanted in the world — and which thus far she has found reasons to deny him. A child.

Perhaps Amber was as much barrier as glue.

Always scared by the prospect of parenthood — the responsibility, the expense, the commitment, the pain — Ruth is suddenly overcome by an even greater fear: that of there not being something 'shared' between them. She knows there is no logical reason for her to be concerned; Ben isn't going to leave her because Amber has died. And isn't it ridiculous to imagine that the animal had become pivotal to their life together? But she can't help herself. The next time they go to the supermarket they will not walk down the pet food aisle, their final bill will be considerably smaller. In itself it is nothing — and yet it is everything.

"Let's see," she says, ruling nothing out. And perhaps for the first time, not even that which Ben wants above all else.

Last Orders

This is the part of the day I like the best; sitting here, all the punters and staff gone home, most of the lights off... Switching off the lights is a bit like switching off the noise. I sit here and scan the bar, the optics, the gleam off the glasses, and sometimes marvel about how frantic it has been. Non-stop for best part of five hours.

And for what?

A glass of single malt (the good stuff, not that rubbish I ladle out to those that know no better) and a few quid in the till. Hardly seems worth it. Especially since takings have been so dramatically down. I did the numbers the other day. Negative nearly forty percent. I asked my accountant where the survival threshold was. Told me it was minus thirty-two.

Well then.

If anyone asks I'll blame Covid. An obvious scapegoat. I mean, everyone suffered — and everyone knows everyone suffered. Sympathy's cheap, especially when we're all feeling the pinch. Two pints instead of three. Might not seem much, but it all adds up — or doesn't. All those pints no-one's drinking any more.

The brewery had been understanding at first, I'll say that for them. They're not known for their compassion. But when the whole industry's in pain they have to try and hang-on in a few places. I used to assume one of them would be here.

But then we had that fracas with those lads up for the races; drinking beforehand, and then straight in after 'the lucky last'. Skinfuls already. I wouldn't normally have served them, but... Needs must and all that.

I wonder if Roger saw the knife before they laid into him. He was always mouthy; got him into more than one scrape. But that day? Bad luck I suppose. His obviously — and mine subsequently. It's difficult to shake off a reputation, even when you don't have one.

Anyway, one more for the road — and in a very real sense this time. Then switch off the rest of the lights. Need to be up early in the morning for the movers.

Poor Holly

Looking at the almost empty coffee cup, he had become transfixed by the way it was reflecting the scene around him. Although the stoneware had been glazed in a glossy ruby tone, the images with which he was presented — behind him, to his left and right — appeared faithful to their source colour. Expecting at least a shading of red in the reflections, when he found them unadulterated he had been forced to turn in his chair simply to validate their authenticity.

It was in that motion — brief and inconsequential — that he may have unconsciously made note of her.

On returning his gaze to the cup, had you immediately interrogated him as to what he had just seen, asked him to detail everything he remembered from that two-second glance, what would he have said? Almost certainly he would have switched from sight to memory and fore-knowledge, after all he went there often enough to be able to describe the layout of the counter in some detail, to relate the way the specials were written on the blackboard — that rather unique script Lou had! And then perhaps he would tell you about the layout of the tables, the benches against the far wall, the high stools in the windows. But people? He might have been able to recall those he had seen on entering (guessing whether or not they were still there), but other than that? "A couple of people sitting in the window" may have been the best he could conjure — conjure being the appropriate verb given he was attempting a minor magic trick.

But if he *had* sufficiently taken her in by looking long and hard just as his mother used to tell him not to — "don't stare, Lex!" — and registered her as an individual, how might he have described her then?

Unremarkable. She was, to all intents and purposes, an anonymous individual: mid-forties, slightly over-weight, wearing a vaguely floral coat which seemed out of kilter with the times. Resting near her feet was a large 'bag for life' — though it was just far enough away to have possibly been left by the previous occupant of the adjacent and now vacant seat. In addition, had he paid any attention to her face, Felix may have been able to deduce something more about her given she was looking squarely his way.

Yet he did not. Might it have made any difference if she had been half her age, slim, attractive, sexily dressed? Almost certainly. But even having said that, Felix wasn't really in the mood to focus on anything frivolous just then. With time to spare before he caught his bus home, he had decided to take the opportunity for a coffee, and this café — although part of a chain — was infinitely preferable to anything on offer at the bus station. It wasn't that he was particularly thirsty, but there was a great deal to think about, to decide upon, and sitting quietly drinking coffee had always helped his thought process.

Not that the problem he was facing was a uniquely knotty one. Indeed, people make decisions about relationships all the time. If most decisions related to ending them, then only a minor proportion concerned their starting — yet it was a challenge of this ilk Felix was facing. He felt recognising the novelty of his situation bestowed upon him some small credit. Recent analysis had led him to the conclusion that, in the majority of cases, people simply 'fell' into relationships, triggered by a chance meeting, a common interest, or too much alcohol. If he were to thus categorise his previous romantic experiences (something which he had indeed done over recent days) he found he could filter them accordingly and, having done so, make conclusions about which catalyst was most likely to offer a modicum of success in the future. But his present dilemma — in the shape of Holly — fit both none and all of those categories at the same time. They had met by chance at an evening pottery course (which ticked the 'similar interests' box), and if, over diner a few nights later, they had indulged in the extra bottle of wine Felix had contemplated suggesting, then the third criteria might also have been met. As it happened, he did not suggest it nor did Holly request it. Without that alcoholic impetus they had subsequently established a kind of equilibrium which rooted them in a romantic 'no-mans-land' — that is until Holly's recent ultimatum delivered to him just six days earlier.

At their pottery class she had told him how she felt about him and informed him that, if he were of the same inclination, she would happily 'take things further and see what happened'. Whether or not the vague surprise Felix expressed at her declaration was genuine, his alarm at her corollary most certainly was: "and if not, then I am giving up the class and most likely you'll never see me again." Perhaps above all else, it was the black-and-whiteness of Holly's declaration which took him aback the most. He had never seen her so definitive; in his experience she seemed a flexible and fluid person, both in how she behaved and in the pottery she created.

"But that isn't necessarily a good indicator is it?"

Woken from his reverie, Felix looked up from his ruby-red cup to see the woman in the floral coat standing by his table.

"I'm sorry?"

"Appearances can be deceptive, can't they? 'Still waters run deep' and all that."

Felix tried to ignore the woman's benign smile and, just as he was composing a suitable put-down, she asked if she could sit with him — and then did so, not waiting for his reply.

"Clichés and platitudes hardly help either, don't you agree? But at least they give one something with which to fill the time while you're trying to come up with the killer line." She chuckled to herself, then sat back slightly.

Wondering whether she was expecting him to deliver such a line, all he could manage was a second "I'm sorry?"

"No need to apologise. It can be difficult, I know. 'Affairs of the heart'." Another chuckle. "It was ever thus… And please don't say 'I'm sorry' again; it doesn't become you. If that's the way you go about things it's no wonder you're struggling to make a decision about poor Holly."

"'Poor Holly'?"

The woman straightened in her chair.

"You know, I think we're going to have to find a way to get you out of this annoying habit of thinking you're keeping up your side of the conversation simply by apologising or asking questions. In the first place, I don't think it moves us along very much, and in the second, it's really annoying."

Felix immediately concocted multiple responses — "what habit?", "what conversation?", "move 'us' to where?" — but recognising all of them for what they were, *and* having been chastised for asking too many questions, he chose to surface none of them. Instead he tried to make a fist of being definitive.

"Look, I've no idea who you are, nor why you've interrupted me like this. And I'm at a loss to think how you could possibly know me or anything about me."

"Or Holly," the woman said.

"What?"

She let the question pass. "Or Holly. You forgot to say that you're also at a loss as to how I know anything about Holly."

"Which is true." Felix ran a hand through his hair. "Given a few extra seconds I'm sure I would have come up with that one too."

The woman chuckled yet again. "Indeed, I'm sure you would have."

"You must be a friend of hers; that's all I can think. But I don't see how that gives you the right... Unless she asked you..." Various scenarios popped into Felix's head, the resulting combination of which was merely to slow down both thought and speech.

"It was very clever what you did there," the woman said, relaxing again into her chair. "You asked questions by making statements, forcing me to counter or confirm them."

"I did?"

"Yes, of course. So, before I answer them, would you like another coffee?"

Instinctively Felix checked his watch. There were still almost twenty minutes before his bus. He was about to respond only to find that the woman had already called the waitress over and was placing their order: "a cappuccino for Felix, and I'll have a flat white. Thank you."

Felix watched the server retreat to the counter, relay the order to the barista, then move on to another customer.

"So," her voice brought him back, "you can call me Angela. And yes, I do know Holly and therefore, knowing Holly, I know about you. How could I not?" She delivered her own question as if it were so self-evident she was amazed he hadn't seen the connection himself.

He felt a little like a young child being explained something in the most rudimentary terms possible.

"I still don't see…" He was going to protest again about her interruption, to ask what she knew about him, what business she had intruding into his affairs.

"Not that Holly knows I'm here," Angela interjected, as if intercepting his thoughts. "This is my own initiative" — she seemed to play with the word — "my attempt to help out a friend."

"And how do you propose to 'help out'?"

Just then the waitress returned with their drinks, Angela breaking from the conversation for a moment to ensure the appropriate pleasantries were observed.

"To get you to a decision, obviously. I think Holly was worried which way you might jump as it were, and now she fears you're not going to jump at all." She paused for effect. "Five days, Felix; you've had five days. And it's the pottery class tomorrow, and from where I sit you're not where you need to be."

"Where I need to be?"

"There you go again!" She shot him an exasperated look. "In terms of making a decision, of course. Your relationship with Holly. So I have decided to help you to come to one. My initiative. As I said, Holly doesn't know I'm here. I'd like to think I'm doing her a favour; looking after her interests.

Because — to be frank — if you turn up to the class still undecided… Well, that's hardly fair on her."

It wasn't what Felix wanted to hear, but he knew Angela was right: he had been vacillating, attempting to weigh-up all the options, go through an ever-expanding list of pros and cons in order to get to the justifiable answer. Always assuming there was one. He nodded to himself. It was an almost imperceptive move of his head. Almost.

"Well then." Angela leant forward. "I want you to forget everything you've been thinking in terms of Holly and your situation, all those questions and counter-questions you've been wrestling with."

"But if I'm going to make the right choice…" It was a weak plea and he knew it.

"Right. Wrong. Where I come from we have some very clear guidance about those."

"Where…"

Angela cut him off. "But that's irrelevant here. Your choice, Felix, isn't between 'right' and 'wrong'; rather it's a question of whether or not you want to make a go of things with Holly. Sorry to be so monochromatic about it, but that's how things stand. There is no safe middle-ground. That's what she's left you with, isn't it?"

He nodded then looked down at his fresh coffee, surprised to find that this time the cup was a deep blue.

"Holly has a preference, obviously — but I can't tell you what that is because it will only influence your decision. Or confuse you even more. Agreed?"

Felix nodded again then lifted the cup to his lips.

"So here's the deal. Before you put that cup back down on the table and then run for your bus, you are going to decide. Right here, right now." Angela spotted the look of panic in his eyes. "It's the only way. This dithering has to end — for Holly's sake."

Wanting to nod again, all Felix could do was to take a sip of his coffee. The cup seemed strangely welded to his fingers.

"Ready?" Angela's face was suddenly stern; she was sitting bolt upright in her chair.

Confused both by the sudden weight of the cup and his inability to put it down — no matter how much he wanted to — all Felix could do was agree.

"I am."

"Felix," as Angela spoke it seemed to him as if all other sound had been sucked from the café, that it was just the two of them sitting there, her eyes resolutely fixed on his own. "What is the answer to Holly's question? How do you feel about her, right here, right now? Are you going to join her on the next phase of her life, or not? What is your heart saying, Felix? What is it telling you?"

No matter how hard he tried not to, Felix remained convinced there was a right answer. Surely there had to be. He had spent his life chasing right answers, why should this instance be any different? Did his heart know? How could it? And what did that mean anyway? Not able to be certain that one of the options was 'right' — in his 'heart of hearts' — he was only left with the other.

"No."

Suddenly his fingers felt entirely disconnected from the coffee cup, and he only just managed to relocate it in its saucer without dropping it.

"Well." Angela let out a brief sigh, relaxed her body. "Holly will be disappointed, but she'll understand. She has always been an intelligent soul. She'll mend."

There was something in the way Angela uttered 'soul' which sounded odd to Felix, as if she was able to invest in it a meaning far beyond his comprehension.

"Now we must be getting on." Angela was suddenly up and out of her chair. "I've got one more chore, and you've got a bus to catch."

He glanced at his watch. Less than five minutes. Looking up he found Angela was already on her way out of the door. On the table, her untouched flat white was now accompanied by a twenty-pound note. The latter — as if a magnet — had already drawn the waitress over.

"Keep the change," Felix said, rising, "I've a bus to catch."

His bus stop was located in a small line of three across from a parade of shops. After leaving the café, Felix reached the crossing just as his bus appeared around the corner. If the lights on the pedestrian crossing changed in time he would be fine, if not he might miss the bus, especially as there appeared to be no-one waiting for it.

It should have been a split-second decision: gamble on the lights, or gamble on the traffic. Another binary choice.

Some eye-witnesses said that he slipped on the kerb, others that he had been making a dash to cross the road. Certainly he had given the taxi driver insufficient time to avoid him as he tumbled in front of his Mercedes. There had been screams

and chaos. Was it any wonder that in such a moment of
madness no-one spotted a slightly over-weight woman in a
floral coat walking away from the scene, a woman not
carrying a bag of any kind, and one who seemed to melt away
into the background.

What you see in the shadows

The unburnished kettle sits on the front-left ring of the gas hob looking vaguely out of place. It is made of copper, and its subtly beaten surface offers an image of another time. Arts and Crafts perhaps. Having said that, the kitchen is not exactly à la mode; it too has seen better days. The cupboard doors — a kind of muddy cream no longer available in modern retail stores — hang very slightly out of true, and on two work surface corners the veneer has been chipped away. Although you cannot tell from this distance, it is not simply that the kettle remains unpolished, but it has not been warmed for a good while, and were you to lift it from the hob you might be surprised how little water it contains. And perhaps the state of that water too.

A cursory glance might have suggested everything is in order — and then you notice the bread bin, its front propped open, a hint of green in the packaging beyond. Or the unwashed cups and plates sitting alongside the sink, their surfaces pockmarked with a kind of black volcanic residue. Beneath the cupboards, cobwebs are in evidence, and as you allow your eye to scan the room for a second time you notice the detritus on the floor. Whether crumbs or mouse droppings you have no desire to resolve.

Then there is the smell; the tell-tale aroma of ancient cooking fat. It is a strangely claustrophobic smell, and seeking its source you spot a small white dish near the cooker. Unable to see if it is empty, you have no desire to find out, to step any further into the room. You are happy to make assumptions and leave it at that.

It might be prudent at this point to switch on a light or open the blinds to reduce the drain on your torch; but you have already discovered the electricity is off, and the idea of allowing more light into the kitchen to reveal all you cannot yet see is unappealing. Irrational or not, you suspect the curtains might fall apart at the slightest touch. They are not particularly substantial.

When your phone vibrates it makes you jump. You take it from your pocket and tap the screen. An email you can leave until later. Part of you wishes it might have been something serious, urgent; something demanding you to retreat back into the hall and out through the front door, back to the haven of the car. You want to drive away without completing your task, the order to 'check the place out'. Neighbours have expressed concern — less at the lack of any obvious movement for some time now, and more at the threat of squatters and what that might mean for the area, for house prices. Replacing the phone in your pocket, you wish you had not come in alone, had not dropped Jack at the top of the road to make enquiries, whistling as he went off up the path to number one. Where is he now? You're in thirteen, six houses away. Surely he must be close. But you know how talkative people can be when they get the chance; you only have to think of your mother and Audrey. They'll soon need their garden fence reinforcing given they spend so much time leaning on it yakking.

If the thought is designed to make you smile, it fails. Instead, you turn back into the hall, look up the stairs, along the corridor to the far room: kitchen at the front, lounge at the back. When had that been 'a thing'? You're not sure. And it doesn't matter. You're simply stalling, listening out for Jack.

Deciding the top of the stairs looks too dark to be ventured alone, you move forward, stepping over a drift of untouched mail and flyers. To your left you see the catch of an under-stairs cupboard; it is not difficult to leave it untouched. Ahead, the door to the lounge is partly ajar. Your feet make the floorboards creak. Had there been squatters they would have flown by now, cascaded down the stairs or bolted past you and out through the front door. Pausing at the sound of the complaining wood, you listen. Nothing. And you suddenly wonder why 'nothing' is more threatening than 'something'. You want your phone to buzz again, for Jack to come through the front door. But there is nothing there either.

You flash your torch around the door, down to the floor. Then, as you take a step towards the room, the beam — for an instant flickering hesitantly — picks out a shape on the carpet. The slippered sole of a foot.

The Engineer

The pub went briefly silent when she walked in, the locals taking her in, head to toe. The path had been wet after all the rain, so she allowed the barman to fixate on her muddy boots for a couple of seconds before heading to the bar. She was used to this staring in bars; what else were men supposed to do?

Finding an unoccupied table in the corner, she smiled as she reflected on the barman's incredulity at her order of Guinness and brandy. That was typical too. It was one of the things she'd come to despise about Peter, his judgement of her, as if there was a standard to which she should conform.

Well, no longer.

She looked around the bar, examining the men there in turn. To see. Just in case. Seduction, pre-nup arrangement, marriage and divorce — or unfortunate accident — money in the bank.

After all, funds were already running a bit low.

Favours

Although Marilyn assured me that he'd 'turned it around', given the depths to which Jed had seemingly sunk it was the kind of statement which required first-hand verification. Not that I was truly bothered. More curious I suppose. So, primarily for that reason — rather than the fact of him being my host at a gathering which, I assumed, was partly to celebrate his resurrection — it was only natural I try and seek him out as soon as I arrived at the party.

Having been told he was 'upstairs', my initial instinct was to try and find him — only to have my path to the upper echelons of his house barred by a couple of his friends standing guard at the foot of the staircase. My reaction was to look up to the first floor landing and wonder in which of the many bedrooms he might at that moment have been demonstrating to Marilyn just how far he'd come. Or how far he was prepared to go. Or then again, perhaps he was basking in his new lease of life and was mid-way through 'initiating' some new unfortunate acolyte. Another notch on the bedpost. Let's be frank, if he'd simply gone for a shit he wouldn't have needed the stairs to be out of bounds.

But as it turned out I'd been wrong about Marilyn's location. As soon as I walked into the lounge I saw her on the far side of the room talking to Geoff or Greg or whatever his name was, plus some other bloke I didn't know. She may have been past her prime and beginning to slide down the other side but, to be fair to her, she could still attract men as if they were wasps and she a pot of jam. She had what it took to come good on a deal too — deals often laced with various sorts of dubious clauses and conditions. If Jed had gone down that route — come up with 'an arrangement' to get Marilyn on-side, batting for him as it were — then you couldn't blame him. The simple fact of the matter was her pronouncing that he'd 'turned it around' *had* to have come at a price — unless his 'self-rescue' was for real of course, something I didn't believe for a minute. Weren't his poodle-Doberman cross-breeds at the foot of the stairs somehow proof of that?

As far as the lady herself was concerned, many had tried their luck using various techniques and wiles (including yours truly) but the majority had fallen at the first hurdle. With Marilyn you knew very quickly whether or not she was interested — and what she was interested in. To be fair to her, she nearly always put your potential and the quality of your work uppermost, especially if she could make money from it. But I couldn't help but feel that what she prioritised was — more often than not — a marginal call. She'd been around long enough to have cultivated a vast network of contacts; one of the standard tropes about her was that there wasn't a door in the industry for which she didn't have a key. It was a joke of which she was undoubtedly aware — and indisputably proud. Yes, she'd given me the odd lead that had led to something, put in a word here and there; but the big gigs, the shows and ads where the real money was to be made were strictly off-limits. Perhaps that's what George or Gary and the other fella were doing, making their case, giving her their best pitch. Perhaps they were a double act of some persuasion; words and music, that kind of thing. Or perhaps they were just chatting about the weather or the state of the economy — though I doubted Marilyn did 'chatting', not without an underlying motive.

Having now located the two people I expected to see (one virtually as it were) I scanned the room for other familiar faces before heading off to the kitchen where I knew the booze and a greater concentration of bodies would be located.

Apart from Marilyn and her two interlocutors, the largest space in the house was in fact sparsely occupied. There were couples on both sofas, a small cabal of three standing by the unlit log burner, and two women engaged in what seemed an earnest conversation near French doors which led out onto a small patio, the house's only meaningful outside space. I recognised some of them. Frank (on one of the sofas) had pipped me for a series of ads for a well-known brand of paint; and I'd worked with Helen (who was sitting on the other) over an exceedingly long weekend during which we sacrificed ourselves to a weird experimental play in some dive in deepest East London. It would have been better had it been the West End, but beggars and all that. Both acknowledged me as I hovered there: Helen waved conspiratorially as if I was in on some joke that was being kept from her partner on the settee; Frank offered a smile that was both condescending and galling. How was I supposed to acknowledge that?

Between the lounge and kitchen was a bijou dining room where the table was part laid out with various snacks and nibbles in matching bowls and plates, the same set Jed had been using for years (though he had long since stopped boasting that they had originated from Heal's). From the general air of devastation it was all too evident that, in spite of the thinly populated lounge, the locusts had already descended, presumably to then move through to the kitchen to savagely attack the drink in a similar fashion. I tugged the bottle of Chilean Merlot from my coat pocket and held it in front of me as if it were my entry ticket. Momentarily placing it on the table so that I could divest my coat onto a pile of other garments atop a couple of the dining chairs, I tried unsuccessfully to see if I could tune-in to any voices in the kitchen hubbub. As with many such events it sounded as if that was where the real action was.

Yet this too was to prove a false assumption. There were only seven or eight partygoers there, the volume of noise they were generating entirely disproportionate to their number. Perhaps it was the drink talking. In theory the evening had not long begun, so if that was indeed the case then they must have been going at it hard. Disheartened both by the noise and the fact that I didn't recognise anyone, I liberated what appeared to be a clean glass — a large clean glass — unscrewed the lid on my Merlot and poured myself a not insignificant measure.

Back in the lounge, I was gorging on a cold sausage roll salvaged during my return journey from the kitchen when Marilyn detached herself from Bill and Ben and made a bee-line for me. Ignoring the fact that I was munching and had both hands full (the wine plus another of the disappointing pastries), she gave me a perfunctory hug and a peck on the cheek, one I was unable to return.

"Dreadful people," she said, her voice just a trifle too loud.

I glanced to where the couple concerned were still talking to see whether her statement had registered. Apparently not.

"Begging favours?" I nodded in their direction.

"Isn't everyone?" There was a twinkle in her eye which made it very plain that she was in no mood for any further such overtures, and that if I'd had anything of that sort in mind I could forget it. Marilyn had multiple ways of conveying messages. She looked down at my glass. "That's a monster, Bruce!" Not shy of innuendo, she could be knowingly crass when she wanted to. "I wouldn't mind getting my hands on something that size."

I laughed dutifully. "You'll need to be quick, I think most of the glasses have already been sullied by the crew in the kitchen."

"Then they can just wash one up for me."

As she made to move in the direction of the dining room, I stopped her. "Have you seen Jed?"

"This evening you mean?"

I nodded.

"Briefly." She leant in and lowered her voice. "He's upstairs."

"Yes, I know. I was hoping to have a word before all this got out of hand." I looked round the room and was suddenly unsure how it would be possible for such a placid gathering to become unhinged. Watching Marilyn do likewise, I imagined her running through some rapid calculation to try and divine whether there was any prospect that she might get something worthwhile out of the evening. If so, it was a process over almost as soon as it had begun. I had a bet with myself that she'd have one small drink and then be gone.

"Audition," she said without any attempt to camouflage exactly what she meant.

"Ah. There's a surprise."

"He says there is a small opening on one of his new projects, something tailor-made for an aspiring young actress."

"So he's up there exploring a small opening."

Although I wasn't surprised by her sudden guffaw, for a brief moment it silenced the room. Heads turned.

"You're wicked!" she announced, and then was gone.

Turning to the rest of the room's occupants I raised an eyebrow, shook my head slightly. It was intended to convey "Marilyn! What's she like?" Seeing it greeted with one or two smiles and a laugh from Helen (as well as a stoney-faced nothing from Frank) I knew I'd carried it off reasonably well. And then the moment was gone — which forced me to consider my next move.

Whether or not I had undertaken a similar assessment to Marilyn I couldn't be sure, but I already felt the evening was certain to be something of a let-down. Looking around the lounge I knew one option was to force myself into a conversation currently on-going; or I could have followed Marilyn into the kitchen to see if I could ingratiate myself there. A third option? There wasn't really a third option unless I went to loiter in the hallway and wait for Jed to reappear, though the two minders at the foot of the stairs hadn't appeared people with whom to chat. Was it that important I spoke to Jed this evening anyway? I had — in Marilyn's parlance — come to ask him 'a favour'. Work had become somewhat sparse and, given he was flavour-of-the-month once again, there was a real possibility that he might know someone who was looking for someone… Indeed, didn't his 'audition' prove exactly that? Amongst other things. And wasn't that partly how things worked and wheels were oiled? However, it took me no more than a second or two to deduce that, whatever opportunities he might be aware of, he was unlikely to be in the mood for serious discussion once returned to the ground floor. He had guests who would require his attention, and there was a certain degree of vacuous professional smooching to be undertaken, jokes to be told, empty promises to be made. My connection to him was reasonable — but not strong enough to trump that, especially if he reappeared in triumphant mood.

I looked down at my glass. Two swigs and it would be empty; one, if I wanted to push it. I thought about retrieving the rest of the bottle from the kitchen but knew most of it would have gone already. I decided on a single swig and then planned to beat as inconspicuous a retreat as I could manage, back out into the night for the walk to the tube.

"Thirsty?" Frank's question, delivered just as I was finishing the dregs of my wine, made me jump.

I turned toward him and tried a half-smile. He had always been a sour kind of character; even when he was happy it was difficult to tell.

"Not really." I looked for somewhere to put the glass down. "I really came to see Jed, and given he's 'indisposed' thought I'd make a run for it; it doesn't look like this party is going to be particularly inspiring."

Frank nodded — though it was difficult to tell whether he was in agreement with me or disapproving of my planned escape.

"Before you go," he began, then started another sentence. It was the way he spoke. "I'm glad you're here actually. Been meaning to get in touch, you know since."

"Oh?"

"Just a quick. One question, if I may."

"Go ahead." I edged toward the dining room as I spoke, both to retrieve my coat and to suggest to Frank that he was on borrowed time.

"Work's been a bit slow because. Just wondered if you knew of anything. On your grapevine, as it were."

Even if it was no more than toadying, I was almost flattered that Frank imagined I might have anything resembling 'a grapevine'; it was flattery supplemented by the somewhat crude satisfaction that he was asking me for help.

"Paint job not working out?"

"End of the series. Cut the last two they'd planned. Not quite hitting the mark, apparently. You've seen them?" There was a note of desperation in his voice.

"Maybe just the one, I think." I made a show of giving his question some consideration, remorselessly wanting to suggest that his ads had been forgettable. Anything to make him feel worse. In truth, they hadn't been that bad; perhaps a little off target, but not by much. "And anyway, I'm not the one you should be talking too. Marilyn's the queen of leads, talk to her." I slipped into my coat.

"Not in the mood," Frank said. "Tried, but you know. Made it plain."

"Didn't stop those other two trying."

"Them? They were pitching rather than digging."

"Really?" For a moment I wondered whether I'd been too hasty in making my decision to leave. If they had an idea for something then sooner or later surely they'd be looking to cast in some form or other. "Anyway, it's probably just as well you didn't try to tap her up. She made it clear to me that she wasn't in the mood to be dishing out 'favours' — not that I was asking of course."

"You're not looking?"

I moved back into the lounge and noticed that Marilyn's two 'pitchers' were no longer present; then I headed for the hall. The two guardians were now sitting on the stairs talking — and Frank was still in my wake.

"Me?" I brushed off the notion. "Not at the moment. Just came round to congratulate Jed on his new projects, you know? But given he's incommunicado… Anyway, let me know how you get on; you know, if you hear of anything. I'll do the same."

Standing outside on the pavement — at least two hours earlier than I'd planned to be — I looked up and down the street. The evening, although short, had been a complete waste of time. By the time I got back to my flat it would be too late to do anything worthwhile other than have a nightcap and hit the sack. I hadn't been able to see Jed; the brief encounter with Marilyn had served no purpose whatsoever; and I'd made no new contacts — not that I'd tried. Under different circumstances I might have made more of an effort, but… Well, you get a sense of how things are likely to pan out. And then, as if to prove my point, the pointless prince of the paint charts had tried to tap me up. He must have been really struggling.

As I started walking I realised that I had no idea whether or not Frank assumed I was being sincere — and then, with a slight smile, also realised that either way I didn't really care.

what's your pleasure?

if they consider us at all most people think we do it because we're wired that way kinky insatiable or that we're mercenary bitches just in it for the money or we're hopeless cases who spend our lives on our backs in order to feed some other kind of addiction

you know the stereotypes

and you know some of them are right because a few of the girls are addicted in one way or another or they're brutally commercial and have a grand plan that revolves around getting enough money to be able to do something else live the life they really want to live their best life and for that reason it's all dispassionate calculation

come to think of it it's pretty dispassionate for all of us

see what i did there

but there are those who do it because we've no choice in this male-dominated society where men call all the shots and women struggle to have a say or make a mark though there are some who do obviously but they're in the minority and have something else about them something in addition to their bodies or other than their bodies and good luck to them i say but that's not the case for the rest of us the silent majority

so some of us do it for a kind of quiet revenge wanting to see if we can grab a slice of the pie however small and not just money either because there's a kind of power shift involved when you're on the job

yes we can get knocked about a bit and we're paid for being whores and there's no glory in any of that but there comes a point where we're in control when no matter how high-and-mighty the punter might be they rely on us to service them and give them what they need or what they're prepared to pay for

and a man is never more vulnerable than when you're holding his dick in your hand

it's fleeting of course this moment of control of euphoria and under the circumstances you might regard it as a different kind of orgasm i suppose because we sure as hell aren't chasing the traditional one but in that moment when you know you're in charge there is something to cling to in addition to the money they leave

of course in the past some of the girls have taken that power too far let it go to their heads the control thing and so there are stories gruesome stories of dicks being dislocated somehow even bitten through though the girls responsible aren't around here any more to say what happened indeed they aren't around anywhere any more so for all that talk of control and power and revenge and the opportunities presented if you're going to make the most of it then you have to be careful and take it to the edge but no further just far enough to give the punters an inkling that one false move and they could be in real trouble

not that i would obviously

sorry there's the buzzer

Hello Honey, what's your pleasure?

Ecdysis

As a young man Ray had always felt old, the consequence of which was, as he aged, he liked to tell himself that at some point he would begin to feel younger; his would prove to be a life lived in reverse, recompense for never having had much of a childhood — at least not one he recognised as such. Yes, he had been smaller, worn shorts, gone to school, scuffed his knees; but all these were events that belonged to the physical Ray, not what he regarded as his 'inner self'. "You were born middle-aged" an ex-girlfriend said just before she left him. Had he not agreed, he might have been minded to put up a fight to keep her.

On the other hand, Louise had never felt like an adult; nor had she any desire to. She couldn't see the point. If her philosophy was reinforced when their paths crossed — post Ray's aforementioned ex-girlfriend — she didn't say. Nor did she particularly care, not at a philosophical level. She believed life should be lived as if there was a fuse burning, one whose length was unknown. The consequent fatal explosion might occur tomorrow or the day after, so as far as she was concerned being an adult consisted of futile planning for a future that might not last days, never mind years. If anyone started talking about pensions within her earshot (admittedly a rare event!) she would burst out laughing or fly into a rage, largely dependant on how much she'd had to drink.

They were, therefore, fundamentally incompatible. Nominate any spectrum and you would find them at the polar ends of it; posit any argument and they would be found in opposing camps. On the face of it they should have been like two circles on a Venn diagram — but circles with next to no overlap. Yet there was something in the theory of opposites' attraction which applied to them; they should not have been drawn to each other, yet were. And desperately so. It was as if each filled a gap in the other; as if they were able to share some surplus in their dominant trait with the other — being adult, being carefree — in order to help complete them, make them more 'rounded' human beings. Their friends — who inevitably belonged to different milieux — were nevertheless consistent in their assessment that, when they were together, almost blending into each other, their amalgamation created a being of considerable force. It was as if they became a strange two-headed animal, an example of the best of all worlds; a beast those same friends christened as 'Louray', their two names conjoined. When discussing upcoming parties or events people would ask "Are Louray coming?" or "Is Louray coming?", never quite being able to resolve the vocabulary associated with the multiple-entity unit.

Even if the area of their Venn diagram overlap was relatively small, it was highly charged. It exuded a kind of power, a life all its own. Given their divergent personalities, logic suggested it should have been a danger zone, and yet in the beginning it was their driving force; it didn't become toxic until much later. Ask them about that initial lure and Ray would probably confess how he'd been mesmerised by Louise's zest for life, the way she would grasp at experience ravenously, without caution. It was evidence of a bravado built from supreme self-confidence; at least that was how the fundamentally insecure Ray saw it. Where he was predisposed to worry about the future, her disregard for safety, security, and probity astonished him. And for her? In Ray she saw someone who navigated through life with a certainty born from patience and calculation. Yet in translating this certainty into terms to which she could relate, she unconsciously interpreted it as a disregard for the burning fuse which so terrorised her; she inverted Ray's caution to become its complete opposite, and did so in such a way to enable her to feel something kindred about him. In a profound way they were each jealous of the other.

It was on this basis that they coexisted symbiotically for the best part of four months. They had crashed together — both metaphorically and literally — quite by accident at the National Gallery one Sunday afternoon. Ray had been typically frustrated by the crowds, the tourists; Louise annoyed at how slowly people moved around the place. If they had been spinning inside the Hadron Collider at CERN, surely their explosive fusion — a physical coming-together in front of a Kandinsky — would have resulted in the discovery of a new particle of such magnetism as to weld them together though without anyone being able to understand why. The collision spawned coffee and later morphed into dinner. After that? Ray phoned into work sick the following day; Louise stayed away from her job too, but didn't bother to call. When they returned to their respective employers on Tuesday their colleagues would not have been unduly challenged to spot a change in them — even if they were unable to define the nature of that change or what had caused it. Louise and Ray saw each other every evening for the rest of that week; spent the next weekend together including a joint appearance at a party thrown by one of Louise's friends. Within a month (before the end of March) they were beginning to discuss plans for summer holidays, having fun trying to collaborate on a suitable agenda given they were coming at the project from opposite ends of the spectrum. What did they settle on? It hardly matters given the holiday was never taken.

The first crack appeared during what had become their innocuous weekly visit to the supermarket, one of the compromises made by Louise to humour Ray's predisposition for routine; there was a similar tally kept in balance by concessions on his side. He had been standing by their semi-filled trolley at the end of the biscuit and chocolate aisle as Louise scooted away from him to pick her confectionery indulgence for the week. As he watched her choosing between Mars, Twix, and KitKat — and knowing she would come back with two of the three — he suddenly found unbidden questions front-and-centre before him as if he too now needed to make a choice. Was this a picture — in microcosm — of his future? And if it was, how did he feel about it? Since meeting Louise he hadn't really considered how his life might be transitioning, nor what into. Before she crashed into him, he had been on a steady if unremarkable track of a slow progress centred around work. Since her intervention, the future had felt like another country, Louise teaching him how to live in the here-and-now. But now there was this intrusion, one of his old habits breaking cover and whispering "remember me?"

He was slightly subdued for the rest of their expedition, and for the remainder of the day too. Having asked himself those questions, he knew he was obliged to answer them as best he could.

So, an image of his future? If that meant doing the same thing ad infinitum — ' the weekly shop' — then, although shopping for food was a necessity, he wasn't sure he couldn't see Louise being happy in such a repetitive scenario over the long-haul; being who she was, at some point surely she would rebel. On that basis, who was he kidding if not himself? Soon the novelty would rub off, and knowing the kind of person she was, that might not be too far away. Yet putting that to one side — and believing that she loved him and that they needed each other, to be together — the second question, how he felt about their future domesticity if indeed represented by the cookie-cutter shopping expedition, remained a valid one.

Fundamentally he was okay with the prospect, but possibly only because he could see no choice, no practical alternative.

Did Louise notice the difference in him, the confusion into which he had unexpectedly thrown himself? Had she spotted the microscopic crack he had uncovered in the dam wall of their relationship? Or was she conscious of other, not unrelated cracks, appearing too? She had scooted away from Ray and the trolley that day with more enthusiasm than usual not because she was desperate to choose chocolate, but rather because she was desperate not to, overwhelmed by a sense of pointlessness in doing so. She told herself she loved Ray (something she had been doing with increasing regularity) and that the price to be paid — like the weekly shop — was just minor inconvenience in the grand scheme. But her demons were returning too.

Gradually the cracks widened, invisibly at first, each of them unconscious of those identified by the other, assuming the fault-lines lay entirely on their side. But within a couple of weeks they became too significant to disguise any longer, and try as they might these embryonic fissures proved impossible to paper over.

Perhaps she was only being true to her natural character when Louise forced the cracks open. Perhaps she had been driven to do so because she recognised where they were heading, how irreparable the dam wall had become. In the space of a few days she excused herself from the shopping trip and then attended a party given by one of her friends without taking Ray along. 'Louray' had reverted to 'Lou'.

He had no way of fighting back. Where Louise's natural instinct was to live life outwardly, his was the opposite — something which provided her with both the opportunity and inclination to escape. Ray's retreat could only be inward, back toward the person he had been that day at the National Gallery. This time their rending sparked no fireworks, no generation of new and mysterious atomic particles, just the sad inevitability of a separation driven by Louise's rediscovery of her old self. Yet if it felt like liberation to her, then in a strange way, it proved a relief for Ray too. Left alone in his flat, he found himself rejoicing that he no longer needed to adopt the persona he'd acquired in order to keep up with her, allowing himself to revert to the quiet, slightly curmudgeonly introvert he'd always been. And with that regeneration, he permitted himself to feel old again. It was like re-inhabiting a previously cast-off and much loved skin.

Orange

She has asked him what his favourite colour is.

"Do I have to have one?"

"Everyone has a favourite colour."

He ponders the assertion for a few moments.

"I know what it used to be," he says.

"'Used to be.' I don't think that counts." She waits for him to respond, and when he doesn't says, "Well, what did it used to be?"

"Orange," he replies, trying to sound definite, concerned he is failing miserably. "For a while at least. But it wasn't really practical."

"Because you're not Dutch?" She laughs remembering how much he said he liked football.

"Not a good colour — professionally that is." He pauses. "Not many orange ties — or shirts come to that."

"Gives the wrong image?"

He nods.

"So what about now?"

"Now?"

"What colour was the last tie you bought?"

He tries to imagine himself in his bedroom, looking at the tie-rack hanging in the wardrobe. Seeing a mainly blue wash he chooses not to confess as much. That would give the wrong impression too. And first — or second — impressions are important.

"Green," he says eventually. It is only a small white lie. At least he possesses a green tie, one he would happily show her should she ever make it into his house, his bedroom. "Nothing too flash. Dark. Classy. Goes well with a grey suit, white shirt."

He leaves the picture there and picks up his glass from the table, the wine having lost some of its chill.

"You can tell a lot about a man from the clothes he wears," she offers, "ties especially."

"You think so?"

"I do. But I'm not too sure about green…"

Reading the cards

He looked at his hand and wondered whose it was. Not that it was artificial; nor had it been salvaged from someone else and grafted onto the end of his arm. Nothing like that. There was also nothing accusative in his gaze, no suggestion that the hand had been responsible for unspeakable deeds or was a part of his anatomy over which he had no control. Rather, his look was an inquisitive one — 'wonder' in the truest sense of the word. Marvelling at the subtle marbling of his pink skin (which wasn't *really* pink at all!) he bent and flexed his fingers, watched the tendons do their work, the soft palm-side pads between knuckle joints going taut and then puffing out slightly as the hand made its way towards being clenched.

There were lines, obviously. Not merely those at the creases of his fingers where he imagined them as folds in a thin sheet of cardboard, but in his palm too, the lines there supposedly containing the entirety of his future. Once, when returning from Europe, he had contemplated having his fortune told but refrained from doing so because, well, what was the point? Life and love and heart; wasn't that what they were supposed to represent, those three shallow canyons dividing the space between fingers and thumb? And wasn't it all rubbish anyway?

For a moment he once again felt compelled to equate palm-reading with tarot — but then pulled himself up short. There was no comparison to be made: the map in his palm was a unique physical attribute, and how tarot cards fell, nothing but chance. One fixed, one not. If he was inclined to give the predictive edge to the tarot it would only have been because there were more of them, more combinations. Once upon a time he had no idea what they meant other than the obvious ones of 'Death' and 'The Lovers'. Back then such knowledge was at best superficial. His sudden thought made him recall a dreadful James Bond movie, though he struggled to place the actor. There were tarot cards in there somewhere, he remembered that much. Such decks had always struck him as colourful and elaborate, even if he hadn't held a pack in his hands for a very long time.

As if by magic, he recalled a small shop in Barcelona down by the edge of the Mediterranean. It was shop filled with tourist tat including, in its window, various packs of cards: conventional 52-card decks with hearts and clubs, diamonds and spades; Spanish and Catalan packs; and several boxes of tarot. Thinking of Barcelona made him think of that holiday all those years ago, and thus of Marta. He looked at his hand again and wondered whether she might have left an indentation of her own in his skin; whether one of those small lines could have been bestowed on him by her, an indelible mark or legacy. It would be one of the tiny creases in the centre of his palm. She'd had a habit of running a finger round in little circles there, an absent-minded gesture even when they were out walking and holding hands. And wouldn't such a location for her bequest have been appropriate, bisecting his 'love' line?

He wanted to smile, but found himself relaxing his fingers again to see if he could get a little colour back, his skin suddenly seeming to have lost its tone. Perhaps that was only appropriate — fitting-in with an ancient sense of loss. Although he occasionally liked to think of himself as romantic, there was nothing in their parting to even approximate to such. She had not been taken from him in an accident, nor by an incurable disease; she had not left him for his best friend — or for anyone else, come to that. And he had not returned to the UK and abandoned *her*, devaluing their relationship to a holiday romance always destined to fail. Had he tested the tarot cards that day when the two of them peered into the window of the water-front shop, he still wondered what they might have said, whether they would have accurately foretold his future.

§

Not looking where he had been going, he had crashed into her as they were coming out of a cinema near Diagonal late one Sunday afternoon. His apology — delivered via some haltingly inept Spanish — only succeeded in making her laugh. "English is fine," she said, her own accent somewhat cosmopolitan, without the heavy dose of Catalan overtone he had been expecting. She looked Spanish in the same way that a girl on Grafton Street might look Irish, or one on the Royal Mile Scottish.

"I wasn't looking where I was going; I'm sorry."

"Thinking about the film?" They had both emerged from a showing of *Jamón, Jamón* in a small bijou cinema.

"Probably. Or Penelope Cruz." He smiled.

"And how much of it did you get?"

Her turn of phrase — English or American if it had to be labelled as anything — surprised him.

"Some. Though, let's face it, wherever you are — and whatever language you speak — relationships are pretty much the same everywhere aren't they?"

Intended as rhetorical closure, her immediate response — "Are they?" — surprised him, and left him not knowing what to say.

"And where are you going now?" she continued.

199

"Is that so you can avoid bumping into me?" Assuming she was joking, he played along.

"No. So that I can walk at least some of the way with you — perhaps." She left the suggestion hanging for a moment. "After all, the metro station is just round the corner and I'm guessing you're probably going there. At least, that's logical isn't it? And as I'm walking that way too…"

"Actually I was thinking of going for a drink and some tapas before I go back to my flat."

She was to later confess it was the discovery that he was living in the city and not some nomadic tourist which piqued her interest most of all. It proved sufficient to see them meandering towards the sea and, avoiding the crowds near the Rambla, ending up in a small café near the cathedral. Across a small circular table they exchanged names, and where he explained to her that he was on a kind of sabbatical, taking a year out from his Art degree in order to spend time immersing himself in Gaudí before at some point heading up to Madrid and then home via Paris. "Soon?" she had asked. "Not for a while." She asked him where he lived. He told her. "Someone assured me it was fashionable in a cheap, 'shabby chic' kind of way." When she laughed at that, he knew he was lost.

§

She first kissed him the following weekend as they made their way up to Montjuïc in the cablecar. Whenever he replayed the scene he tried — as always! — to persuade himself that he had made the first move; or, as a fallback, that it had been a mutual coming together. He had been standing at the window looking out over the park below when she moved to his side and somehow enveloped him, her arms around his waist, her lips to his. There was something urgent in that first embrace; it was urgency which, on reflection, he decided was one of her defining characteristics. Had it not been, she surely would not have been so forward when leaving the cinema.

The inevitable consequence of her irresistible overwhelming of him was that they remained in contact for the rest of the day; occasionally finding a quiet spot to kiss as they walked down from the castle an hour or so later, their public statement of attachment in the holding of hands — and that little circling motion of her finger in his palm. Was that a statement of intent too, at least on her part? How could it not have been; that was his conclusion now. He was already in thrall of course, but she was from a different culture — presumably a Catholic — and she had only just met him; yet that urgency of hers seemed to trump everything.

Was that when Barcelona truly came alive for him? She seemed to delight in showing him backstreet cafés, the somewhat ramshackle zoo, and was particularly proud of the excavations at El Born. He had seen the Picasso museum by himself three times already, but walking through the galleries with Marta somehow elevated the work; it was as if holding her hand enabled him to get closer to the soul of one of Spain's favourite sons. Rarely seeing her during the week (she quoted family and work) at weekends they would stare at Gaudí and she would give him the Catalan perspective. Although they laughed at the graffiti on a wall near the Parc Güell — *tourists go home* — she was clearly disturbed by it and, for a short while once inside the park, left his side to stare at the flowers and plants alone.

§

"Are you happy?" she asked him one rainy Saturday, a slight catch in her voice.

He had smiled. "Of course. Blissfully. How can I not be?"

What he did not tell her was that his happiness was now graduated, diminishing by a increasing fraction each day. Before he met her in the summer, he had already made arrangements to be in Madrid in mid-January and Paris in April; not just arrangements, but money had changed hands. He had always made reference to having to go there in a casual off-hand manner, but as November turned into early December he found himself counting down in weeks rather than months.

Of course he'd had options: he could choose not to go; he could accept his fate with Marta, give up the monies he had already paid as lost, and try and get an extension on his flat. Or he could take her with him. The latter was an idea he had floated to see if she would be interested in such an adventure, but she again quoted work and family as reasons not to leave the city. He had discovered that her mother was 'unwell' and her younger brother 'troublesome', but that was all. On occasion he wondered if they were the rootstock of her zeal, somehow compelling her not to waste time and energy.

"Then I am too," she had said in response to his rhetorical question, then slipped away into his galley kitchen to make coffee.

But he felt his disquiet growing, as if there was a poison leeching from the travel tickets secreted away at the bottom of his chest of drawers. Yes he was happy, but increasingly it grew to be happiness with caveats, corrupted by the ticking of the clock. And it was spreading too. Even as she made special efforts to ensure that the run-up to Christmas would be memorable, he sensed something changing in Marta too. He worried she might be feeding off his anxiety or, in rummaging through his things, had found evidence of his itinerary.

During December, although they came together slightly less frequently, when they did the collisions were more intense than ever.

Excusing herself based on family tradition and religious rigour, Marta told him she would not be able to see him on Christmas Day but promised to visit the day after. It was an absence which saw him walking the oddly quiet festive Barcelona streets alone, occasionally looking down at his hand and wondering why hers was not there. And he thought about Madrid and Paris, the lure of the Prado, the Louvre, the Musée d'Orsay, and tried to balance those against Marta and the promise of the city he now inhabited. It was as if there was an equation to be solved, the weighing of one against the other — but he had never been very good at maths.

When he returned to his flat he found a small package waiting for him. It had been bound in Christmas paper, the label bearing his name and a single 'x'. He recognised her writing. They had agreed not to give presents. The necklace he had bought her was sitting on his small kitchen table similarly wrapped, and so he decided to wait until they were together before opening her gift. The two presents kept each other company on the table overnight.

They were still there at lunchtime the following day, Marta having not arrived when expected. He tried to get hold of her, but failed. And so they were still there at three o'clock. By five, now certain she was not coming, he opened her gift.

It was a pack of tarot cards. The seal on the box had been broken and three loose cards fell to the table: the Fool, the Wheel of Fortune, the Tower. It was, he was sure, a message of some kind, but he had no idea what — at least not until he spent the next hour researching the internet. The Tower and Wheel of Fortune suggested upheaval, disaster, change and bad luck; he could find nothing positive in them. And the Fool?

Which of the two of them did that represent? Him for believing in her, or Marta for believing in him — or in the cards? Inevitably perhaps, he has always told himself that he had been the fool — and a guilty one at that. Every time he looks at his hand, the palm where her fingers used to circle, he sees in his broken love line the damning evidence.

The Next Bond Girl

In her prime she had oozed sex-appeal. The lustrous black hair she had so carefully cultivated — and which one studio had chosen to temporarily insure — set her aside from those she regarded as 'ten-a-penny' blondes. Her figure, full like her hair, helped too; and the 'whole package' (as some enthusiastic casting directors chose to term it) had been impressive enough for her to be dubbed 'the English Lollobrigida' for a while. If that weren't compliment enough, the fact of her Englishness made her even more alluring, offering a rare combination of self-evident lust and cultural reserve. Few could claim to possess it. Had she been 'Continental', she probably would have been a nobody, especially in Hollywood.

The rumours started not long after she'd had the main supporting role in the critically dubious — but commercially semi-successful — film noir, *Someplace in the Shadows*. Playing the doomed gangster's moll, her character's epiphany — "Seeing the light!", as the trailers portrayed it — was hardly challenging in acting terms, but it provided her with multiple opportunities to toss her curls and lean provocatively into the camera. Although the Bond franchise was in full swing, in 1984 some serious questions about its future were being asked. Many people thought the previous year's *Octopussy* was a turkey — and Connery's unofficial 'Bond Movie' *Never Say Never Again* a whole flock of them. According to those 'in-the-know', they were going to drop Moore because he was too old. Populist wisdom suggested that the franchise needed a new spark — and not just in the eponymous title role.

Someone told her to expect a call.

When she relayed this news to disingenuous friends, they made a point of saying the things they were supposed to — and then behind her back uttered all those they knew she didn't want to hear. Others — arguably more supportive and kindly — wished her well but gently wondered whether she might not be just a little too old.

"Old!" She chased the notion away. "Maudie must have been forty-five if she was a day in that last one. *And* it was her second go round!"

Maude Adams — who she didn't know and had never met — had been thirty-eight or so when *Octopussy* came out, so *she* would be the one pushing forty-five first.

Not that any of that mattered. The rumour was the thing. In Tinsel Town, fairy tales came true.

So for the next few years she did what she could — or thought she should — in order to remain in the limelight: started living a life that was a little more risqué in order to get her photo into the mags and gossip columns; allowed her necklines to plunge lower; lied about her age. It was a process of gradual reinvention, of trying to turn back the clock all the while it was still moving inexorably forward. She still told everyone she was confident Cubby would call any day now. Her knowledgeable English friends were reminded of King Canute.

Keeping Moore on for one last hurrah in *A View to a Kill* and casting the thirty-six year old Tanya Roberts alongside him, she took as a sign: another turkey, another leading lady whose hair and figure she could easily outdo.

When they finally said it was to be Moore's last outing as Bond, she became increasingly certain of her fate, and began scouring magazines for hints as to who her new leading man would be. When they chose Timothy Dalton (who she also didn't know), she saw him as a kindred spirit, linked by their shared Britishness and similar ages — even if she had a few months on him.

She still expected the call.

Inevitably perhaps, the enhanced make-up and daring dresses were gradually supplemented by the odd pill or potion. There were clever doctors who could work wonders — and all she needed was just one single wonder.

When the calls for auditions elsewhere started to dry up, she simply didn't notice, her days structured around ever more elaborate early morning 'getting ready' routines, and then hours topping up her already over-done tan as she waited for the phone to ring. Obliviously sliding into obscurity, most of her friends stopped calling as soon as they knew her agent had. It was as if both her career and her name had already been erased from Hollywood's future.

These days — many years and another Bond later (she has always liked Pierce Brosnan) — the only people who regularly speak to her are her housekeeper, her gardener, and those so-called friends who are prepared to suffer hearing of her inevitable destiny once again, the price they are prepared to pay for leeching off her a little more. Most of all she revels in the occasional strangers who come to call — delivery boys in the main — for whom she flicks her thinning hair and flashes her ageing cleavage, and proudly announces that she is going to be the next 'Bond Girl'.

Diagnosis

"Is she badly hurt?"

"Just a few scratches. She's a bit shocked. That's all."

To Cassie it sounds catastrophic, her brother's unprovoked attack on the nurse tangentially akin to the killers she's seen on *Shetland* and *Silent Witness*. The phone feels hot in her hand and she's unsure if that's just a physical reaction to the news — a sweaty palm perhaps — or whether her Galaxy is one of the ones Samsung has been having trouble with. Years before they'd had a car called a Galaxy and that was always breaking down too, though she blamed that on the reckless way Eddie drove it.

She thinks of the chocolate bar she'd loved as a child.

Jan carries on. "He's quiet again now. I think they gave him something. And they're going to run some more tests."

"They've no idea of the best treatment?" Cassie waits for her sister-in-law to respond. She thinks she hears the beginnings of a sob. "Are you okay?"

"It's hard, Cass." Jan's voice sounds suddenly distant. "They're doing what they can — which I don't think is having much of an effect — but as for these sudden bouts of rage… And he doesn't say much."

"Never did," Cassie confirms. "Tight as a clam, ever since we were kids. Except when he was out with the dogs; chatter away to them about all sorts, but as soon as mam or dad or I got close…"

"Tell me about it."

There is a brief silence; a few seconds in which two lifetimes of understanding and mutual experience are exchanged.

"I may try and pop down at the weekend, just to see him," Cassie suggests.

"That would be great if you could; give me a break."

And then just like that she is committed to visiting her brother again, which probably only meant one thing.

§

Even if the trains aren't that frequent, the journey into Lincoln isn't particularly onerous. What Cassie objects to most is the expense of the taxi that takes her to and from the hospital. On her first visit she tried the walk from the station, and although going via the arboretum was pleasant enough, it started raining on her return and so she arrived back at the station bedraggled. Taking the bus to the station from the hospital on her second trip to see Jimmy had been fine, but when she'd arrived she had taken the wrong one from the bus station and travelled twenty minutes in the opposite direction before she realised her mistake. Hence resorting to taxis.

Finding out from Jan that Jimmy is on the same ward as her previous visit has at least made navigating the hospital corridors that little bit easier. In spite of the coloured lines on the floors and the coded signs, there is still something anonymous about each corridor and intersection. But then she's always found hospitals that way — and she's had more than enough experience of them: first dad then mam, and then — after what seemed like no interval at all — Eddie's heart attack which eventually did for him a week later. And now here's Jimmy: another relative, another hospital, another ward. Who could blame her for fearing the same negative outcome?

"Can I help?" A young nurse with slightly pink hair has arrived at her side.

"I'm fine," she says, slightly flustered at the intrusion. "Visiting my brother. Preparing myself."

"Your brother is?"

"Jimmy. I mean, James McArdle."

Cassie sees a flicker of recognition cross the nurse's face, and can't help but glance down to her arms, her wrists, to see if there are any tell-tale scars.

"Room six," the nurse smiles. "We put him in there the other day. Somewhere he can be quiet."

Knowing that isn't the only reason, Cassie nods then walks through the door the nurse now holds open for her.

§

Jimmy is lying in bed as she enters, his eyes closed. Cassie takes off her coat, lays it across the back of the visitor's chair, then places her handbag on the floor.

"I know you're there."

His voice startles her. Mid-way through sitting down, she continues with the motion, then settles.

"How are you?" She wonders what else is she supposed to begin with.

"You know how I am. I'm dying." There is something abrupt and uncompromising in his voice.

"You don't know that, Jimmy."

"Of course I do; I'm not bloody stupid. They keep giving me pills, taking tests. I've been plugged into this thing" — he waves an arm and the drip tube clicks against its stand — "for weeks now. What's that supposed to mean, eh?"

"Isn't that just saline, to keep you hydrated?" Cassie tries to be upbeat. "I remember…" She stops herself.

"Yes, so do I… But 'take this pill' then 'take that pill'? They've not got a clue. I'm stuck in here like some guinea pig and all the while they're experimenting on me, hoping to land on some magic combination of drugs."

"Have they told you that?"

"They haven't told me anything — which is how I know." Jimmy groans as he shifts himself to be a little more upright in the bed.

Cassie looks away and glances around the room. It too is anonymous, bare, bland. She has seem images of rooms in private hospitals, rooms adorned with pictures and flowers, and can't help but wonder whether such a room would make any difference at all to her brother.

"Did Jan say any anything?"

"About?"

"The bloody weather!" He rolls his eyes. "Me, of course. Have they said anything to her they haven't said to me, something I should know?"

"She didn't say. And how would she know anyway? What you've been told, I mean." The question isn't intended to be rhetorical, but Cassie can tell he has no intention of responding to it. She can only assume that Jan has told her as much as she can. On one level, Jimmy is correct: they're struggling to know how best to treat him. Or fix him. She imagines Hugh Laurie — Dr. Gregory House — walking into the room, leaning heavily on his cane, asking the critical question no-one else had thought of, then concocting the remedy only he could see. But then life isn't like a television series. "What do you want to know anyway?"

"Nothing much. Just when I can get out of here." Jimmy pauses for effect. "Dead or alive."

"Don't say that Jimmy!"

"Why not? It's what everyone's thinking, isn't it? I bet Jan's already checked out the insurance policy." He pauses. Cassie wonders if he knows he has gone too far. "Pass me that water, would you."

Cassie stands, walks to the bedside cabinet where there is a jug of water and a plastic glass one third full. She tops up the glass, hands it to him. He takes a drink, gives her back the glass which she replaces on the cabinet before sitting back down. Although it is only two weeks since she was last there, she can see the change in him. Yes he looks thinner, more drawn, less well in fact — as if the hospital is having the opposite effect to that intended — but there is something altered in his manner too, his tone of voice, every word laced with accusation.

"What about that nurse?"

"What nurse?" Jimmy looks genuinely confused.

"The one you hit."

"I didn't hit anyone," he says, a strange mix of innocence and defiance in his words. "It was a misunderstanding. An accident. She was trying to give me something — more pills, an injection, I forget what — and I just tried to push her hand away. That's all there was to it."

"That's not what Jan thinks."

"Am I supposed to care about that?"

Cassie ignores the implication. "Nor the hospital."

Unsure whether that is the case or not, Cassie tries it as a gambit to get him talking. If he's going to play the bully then perhaps an implied threat might work. Were he to challenge her, she can point to his being alone in this room as evidence. She has her response ready: "Why do you think they've put you in here?" But Jimmy says nothing.

She is suddenly tired.

"Why are you so angry, Jimmy? And don't tell me it's simply because you're not well. I know you better than that."

"Don't you think I have a right to be upset? I've been stuck in here for weeks with no idea when I'm going to get out. Nor what sort of shape I'll be in when I do. That's probably me finished as far as work's concerned…"

"You can't play that card with me! You hate your job. Not going back's more likely to be a relief than anything else." Cassie wonders if that's what she's there for, to pick holes in his arguments. "And yes, you do have every right to feel upset. None of this is very fair, is it? 'Why me?' you might want to know. Maybe even" — she pauses — "why not Jan? Or me?"

"I wouldn't wish this on you."

"I'm not saying you would, just that I'd try to understand if you wished it *was* someone else. Isn't that normal? Isn't that what we did with mam and dad? I know I did when Eddie left me." She is conscious that she has made her husband's death sound like a betrayal — which in a way it was.

They stop speaking just as the door opens and the nurse with the pink hair enters.

"Everything okay?" she asks, looking more at Cassie than Jimmy.

"Yes, we're fine," Cassie replies.

The nurse looks at Jimmy. "Another fifteen minutes and the doctor should be doing his rounds. You know how punctual he tries to be."

"Yes sister," Jimmy says.

The nurse smiles at Cassie. "'Sister' indeed! Will you listen to him!"

Cassie catches a trace of an Irish accent. And then the nurse is gone, the door closing quietly behind her. Cassie wonders about scratches again, whether she had been the one on the receiving end.

"She seems nice."

"They try hard. It's difficult." And then, after a short pause. "It's not her fault."

"What's not?"

"That I'm here." Jimmy looks at the closed door, then across the room to the small window whose blinds are partially closed. "I know I give them a rough time occasionally. I don't mean to, but..."

Cassie waits for Jimmy to look back at her. "But?"

"The frustration's not at me being here. Or at dying come to that — if that's what's going on." He rushes through the last part of the sentence. "I mean, it happens to all of us, right?"

"So what is it?" Cassie chooses not to acknowledge his statement.

"It's what the place has done to me. It's the realisation of what I've missed or didn't do. Of what can't come again no matter how much I might want it to." He pauses. "It's regret, Cass. A lifetime of regrets all suddenly bundled up into one big package… It's as if I woke up here one morning and there it was, sitting at the end of the bed, bursting at the seams. Special delivery."

She had been expecting him to rail against Jan, to complain about how selfish their parents had been as they neared their own end; she imagined him on his high horse about his job, or politics, or religion. He usually has a go at her, too. For as long as she can remember he has been a perpetually disappointed man.

"That doesn't sound much like you," she says disingenuously.

"Who does it sound like?"

"Someone who's feeling guilty — or maybe sorry for themselves."

"What's that supposed to mean?"

"Oh, I don't know." She's certain of the opposite. "When people feel sorry for themselves don't they do so on some kind of superficial level? You know, the 'life isn't fair' brigade. How often are we specific? Or are you being specific, Jimmy?"

She remembers how she felt after Eddie died, how complex her emotions seemed to be. There was guilt somewhere there, but mixed in with that a host of other ingredients: resentment, anger, relief. Having experienced it herself, it's a heady concoction she's happy enough to ascribe to her brother for the moment; it may exonerate him.

"I don't do guilt," he announces. "You tell me what I've got to feel guilty about."

Although she starts compiling a list in her head — their parents, Jan, his first wife, their children, her — she lets his challenge slide.

"I can't help thinking about missed opportunities; you know, those times you should have done one thing but did another. And then later you realise the mistake — and later still, finally recognise you can't go back and fix it. You get that?"

"An example?"

"You want one?"

Cassie nods.

"Once, near the end, when I was having a row with the Old Man about all that inheritance stuff, he asked me to tell him what I thought of him. Straight out. 'Let me have it' he said."

"And did you?" Cassie knows it wouldn't have been pretty.

"No, I didn't. I said nothing. Nothing." Jimmy shifts a little in the bed, reaches for the glass of water himself. "But I should have, I should have. It wouldn't have made any difference in the long run, but he should have known what I really thought."

"You think he didn't?" Then, after a moment, "If you had told him you wouldn't be feeling regret at not having spoken out but guilt at doing so."

"Like I said, I don't do guilt."

The room absorbs Jimmy's words, and from outside Cassie is suddenly aware of a conversation, the sound of shuffling footsteps, the beeping of a nearby machine.

"And that's what's in your 'special delivery'?"

"That. More. Lots of it. It's as if each example is printed on one of those little cards, a neat black frame around its edges."

"Like those inviting you to a funeral," Cassie thinks, remembering the cards the undertaker had printed for Eddie's over-blown send-off.

"And tied round the whole bunch of them, a fancy ribbon. And the whole lot is screaming at me, all the time, when I'm asleep, or just sitting here, or when the doctor comes — or the nurse tries to poke me with a needle."

"What do they scream, Jimmy?"

"That there's no going back. That the unspoken belief we all have about being able to do so, to go round again, to get a second run at things — you know, how we feel we're immortal — is just a gag, a con trick."

Cassie has never felt immortal. All she feels these days is tired. She wonders if she has ever assumed she could go back, do things differently, and concludes she has not. Yesterday was gone, as was the last hour, the last minute, Jimmy's last words. Perhaps there was something worth regretting there.

"And on those cards?" Jimmy allows momentum to carry him along. "That row with the Old Man; how I should never have married Jeanie, nor had the kids; how I should have left Jan years ago — or persuaded her to leave me; how I should have told Wilson that he could shove his bloody job up his arse rather than kowtowing to him. And that time in the hotel in Manchester…" Seeming older than when she walked into the room, he shakes his head. "It doesn't matter."

Unsurprised to hear his regret about Jeanie, Cassie is slightly thrown by what he has said with regard to Jan. She hadn't expected that. And she has no idea what he is talking about when he mentions a Manchester hotel. But what she wants to know more than anything else is whether there's a card with her name on it. And if there is, what circumstance is also etched there. It's Jimmy; how could there not be such a card?

"And me, Jimmy?"

"And you what?"

"Is my name on one of the cards? Or more than one?"

Jimmy reaches for the glass again and takes a sip of water. At that moment the door opens. Not remotely like Gregory House, a tall slightly swarthy white-coated doctor enters with the pink-haired nurse in his wake. Both are smiling their professional smiles. Cassie looks back to Jimmy who, plainly struggling, seems to want to greet them as if they have come to rescue him.

Dust, dancing

"When did you last hoover?" Abby asks as she pauses at the living room door.

"It broke."

"The hoover?"

"Stopped working."

"Really?" She tries to keep the frustration from her voice. "And where is it?"

Her aunt looks round the room as if expecting to see the Vax propped-up in a corner, or perhaps by the sofa as if it were a guest just getting up to pop to the loo or to the kitchen to put the kettle on. "Where it usually is," is what she settles on.

Abby knows nothing is 'usually' anywhere anymore.

Turning into the hall she pauses, then settles on the under-stairs cupboard. That would be the logical place to keep it — not that logic plays much of a part in her Aunt's life now. Opening the oddly-shaped door, she is met by a pile of newspapers at least three feet high and the smell of air inadequately stirred.

"I thought you had the papers cancelled," she shouts over her shoulder, remembering a conversation with Grace about how she would get her carers to speak to the corner shop.

Getting no response, she is about to close the door when she sees the hoover's handle in a corner, half-hidden by two cardboard boxes optimistically labelled 'Xmas decs'. Lifting the boxes into the hall, Abby is able to get some purchase on the vacuum and hauls it out after her. In the light of the hallway she can see that the cylinder is filled to bursting.

"It might not be broken," she says, returning to the lounge holding the machine by the throat as if it was a trophy. Her Aunt looks at her, through her, around her, almost as if she has obtained the ability to travel in other dimensions while remaining physically rooted in her increasingly threadbare armchair. "And I thought you were having the papers cancelled?" Abby says again.

"Papers?" The word seems to rouse Grace. "Haven't seen a paper for weeks. Or months even. That Chrissie spoke to the newsagents — if those are the sorts of papers you mean."

"What other sort of papers are there?" Abby waits for a response. Grace looks toward the window even though the yellowing lace prevents her from seeing into the world outside. "Shall I see if I can get this going then?"

Around three seconds. That's how long she is now prepared to give her Aunt before moving on. It used to be longer; she used to try different ways of asking the same question in order to elicit a meaningful response. But now? Well, what's the point?

She is already in the kitchen when the response finally comes, uttered almost in a whisper, a sound she would have had difficulty hearing even had she still been in the room.

"Doug will fix it when he gets back."

§

Grace is in the kitchen when she hears the front door.

"Is that you, Doug?"

"No, it's Prince Charles. Who do you think it is?"

222

When Doug enters the room she is wiping her hands on a tea towel and smiling. Although it's his standard response, he occasionally varies the personage, just to surprise her. Over the years many people have walked into her house disguised as her husband: the Pope, Idi Amin, Francis Rossi, Bobby Charlton, Henry Kissinger. When she was a little younger she had hoped for Christopher Lee or Roger Moore — and not in the sense of pretend either.

"Bread, self-raising flour, potatoes, butter," he says as he places a shopping bag on the work-surface near the fridge. "Oh, and those scones you like from Benson's. They were reduced given it was towards the end of the day."

"Which means they'll be stale by this time tomorrow." The complaint is manufactured.

Recognising it as Grace's equivalent to 'thank you', Doug smiles and removes his coat. "And I saw Wilf too; you know, from the Working Men's Club."

"How is he?"

"Not doing too well." He leaves the kitchen just long enough to hang his coat on a peg in the hall. "Oh, he says he's fine and all that, but you can tell he's still not got over Ann."

"Well at least he's out."

"If you can call shopping in Tesco's 'going out'…"

"Tea?" Without waiting for a response, Grace turns her attention to the kettle.

Intercepting the implied instruction, Doug unpacks the bag.

"Will you miss me when I'm gone?" It is a question asked almost absent-mindedly.

Grace pauses, the kettle in mid-air on its way to the hob.

"Gone? Where do you think you're going? Not fantasising about that barmaid from 'The Plough' again, the one with the big chest?"

"Vicky?" He chuckles as puts the flour away in a cupboard. "Why would I be doing that?" Opening the fridge to do the same with the butter, he passes her the milk.

"Why wouldn't you, more like! I've heard she's not that fussy."

"Well that's some kind of compliment isn't it?" Doug feigns hurt.

"I meant about older men."

"'Older men'? I could be her father."

"Well then, more credit to you if you could get the daft chump to drop her knickers!"

Doug laughs, knowing they are still okay together.

§

Back in her car, Abby scrolls through the inbox on her phone. She sighs. The unread are mostly from people who seem to want something or to sell something. There are emails from companies she has never heard of, people she doesn't know. How do they get her email address? It seems every time she buys something — in person or on-line — and has to give it out, soon enough she's bombarded by a new wave of the stuff, like rubbish washed up on a beach. If all the emails were real letters in physical envelopes, delivering them would give the postman a hernia. And she's had it drummed into her — by the kids too! — not to click on anything in an email. As a result, she doesn't even trust the 'unsubscribe' link fearing she will be sucked into some nether-world where she'll lose all her money. Not that she has much. Her job and what Gary sends is only just enough to keep their heads above water, especially as it's becoming more expensive to keep the nearing-teenage kids happy.

About to turn the ignition, she sees Mo, one of Grace's carers, walking toward the house. Abby waits, winds down the window.

"How is she?" Arriving at the side of the car, Mo stops, inclines a head towards the house.

"The same. Worse. Who knows? I've just spent twenty minutes unclogging the hoover and then running it around downstairs — not that I got any thanks for doing so."

"I'm sure she would if she could," Mo says.

Abbey pauses, then turns the key. The car grumbles into life.

"Yes, I know. Still..." It is a sentence which requires no finishing. "Must go, otherwise I'll be late picking the kids up."

They nod to each other, then Mo turns into the front garden and Abbey pulls on her safety belt.

§

"What did you mean?"

"What did I mean about what?" Doug looks away from his favourite mid-afternoon game show to where Grace sits knitting.

"About missing you when you're gone."

"You know," he says, uncomfortable that it should need spelling out, "like Wilf and Ann."

"That's what I thought." She gently tugs at her ball of wool to free a little more for her needles. It is a motion which makes Doug think of fishing and how much he misses it.

"Don't you think we should talk about it?"

"I do not, thank you very much."

Doug is unsure whether her tone hides fear or anger. "But there will be arrangements…"

"Well right now I'm not interested in your 'arrangements'. And why should you assume that you'll be done first anyway, especially after the life I've had?" Her complaint makes him smile; 'the downtrodden wife' is standard patter when she's not being entirely serious. "And if you think I'm going to end up like that fruitcake Wilf if you do go first, well, you've got another think coming!"

He looks back to the television. "Glad to hear it." He waits for a contestant to answer another question. "Though it is likely, me going first. Statistically speaking. And I am older."

"*You're* older?" Grace looks across to where he sits. "Well you wouldn't think so gallivanting about with your bowls and darts, chatting up over-endowed barmaids between throws!"

"I had to give up fishing." Wanting to prove his point, this is his only evidence. He'd had a funny turn down at the canal one day. Luckily a couple of dog-walkers had been passing to catch him before he toppled into the canal. Now he is obliged to take his recreation where others are.

"Well you never caught anything anyway — apart from old boots and shopping trolleys."

Coincident with the arrival of the adverts, Doug looks across to where Grace sits, a slight smile on her lips. Yes, they'll be alright.

And they are — until six months later when a heart attack in the dried goods aisle of the supermarket ends Doug's life.

§

The lights at the junction with the High Street are always slow, their brief permission to progress always compromised by someone wanting to turn right and thus holding up the rest of the queue. As Abbey watches a second green light fade, she can't help but wonder how unfair it is that the burden has fallen on her. Oh the carers do what they're paid to do, but they're not the same as family. She wishes her cousins were here to help, but they're ensconced in Falmouth and Truro, the consequence of a wholesale family move to the South West many years ago. She can't remember when they last saw Grace. Or Doug come to that. Five years ago, when they were both still around? Or longer than that?

It is a feeling, this aloneness, which has become her everyday. Yes she has the kids, but they're still too young to be of any use to her in the way an adult needs support. And when Pete and Marcy do ring from Cornwall (increasingly rare events) although she knows they mean well, all their conversations do is reaffirm her isolation. It is a solitude sometimes deep enough to catch her off-guard — like now, as she waits to edge forward — and she finds herself wishing that one day Jack will reappear, tentatively knocking at the front door even though he has a key, and still wearing the ancient leather jacket that has been welded to him from before the day they met. She imagines opening the door and then, once the surprise has left her face, allows a look to be shared between them which is sufficient to erase the previous three years as if they never happened. If that were so, the next time she visited Grace he would be by her side and she'd willingly endure the palaver of reintroducing him — not that doing so would have any long-term value. Abbey knows he would be shocked to see Grace the way she is, find himself knocked a little sideways. But then the old Jack would kick-in, the one she fell in love with, and he'd be charming and engaging, and in spite of herself Grace would be persuaded out off her fragmented shell if only for a few minutes.

But that's as much a fantasy as is her ambition to one day drive straight up to these lights, find them at green, and sail right through. They change again. Three cars make it. Abbey gains a few metres; perhaps she'll get by next time. Then the car in front of her indicates that it is turning right.

She supposes the split wasn't all Jack's fault. Yes, he was the one who strayed, but in moments like this — moments when she wants her part-time wish to come true — Abbey concedes that to some degree she must have given him cause. Certainly he made his feelings on the matter plain enough the Sunday he left. In spite of what he said, of course she wasn't manipulative or over-bearing, and she never bullied him. Maybe she set her sights for him a little too high, the standards she expected him to maintain after the kids came along fundamentally unrealistic. Even so, was that sufficient excuse for him to go off the rails, play fast-and-loose in such a cavalier manner — and especially with that woman from 'The Plough'?

Or were his dalliances nothing more than desperation, a cry for help? Perhaps he didn't really mean some of those hurtful things he said that morning. There is so much she doesn't want to believe is true, or happened, or is happening.

The lights go green again. Abbey engages first gear and edges forward one car-length and stops.

§

"You left the gas on."

"What?"

"I said you left the gas on." Doug appears in the lounge doorway. Grace is fixed on the television. She laughs.

"I don't think so. I always turn it off once the kettle's boiled."

"Or boils dry." Which is what Doug thinks, but dare not say. And anyway, this time it wasn't the kettle.

If Grace's degradation has crept up on them both, he is the only one noticing. As he shuffles back into the kitchen to try and rescue a saucepan which now has something dark welded to its insides, he tries to identify the moment all this started, that first tell-tale incident — and finds he can't. He watched Ann slide away from Wilf, and is seeing signs of Wilf going the same way. You hope it won't happen to you — but more than that, you hope it won't happen to the one you love.

Would the hob being left on have been the first sign? Or the television? The first time Grace said she wanted a cup of tea having only just had one? Or when she couldn't remember Clark Gable's name as they watched *Gone with the Wind* for the umpteenth time? She loved Clark Gable. And though he can't place that moment, that initial instant, he knows it doesn't matter; in itself it signifies nothing. Other than life can be a bitch sometimes. As he watches her these days, sitting glued to the television, he can't help but imagine Grace — his old Grace — slipping away from him, one atom at at time. He imagines those atoms queuing up at the front door, and every time he goes out they run away, and when he returns home he

229

finds her less of the person she was. It makes him want to cry. Indeed, he has cried, both at the unfairness of it and at the fear that the same fate might await him too.

§

It amazes her that she had never noticed how light came through the net curtains. Not merely the way it is filtered, but how — in the places where the net almost turns to decorative lace — it shoots beams into the room illuminating the specks of dust agitated and swirled by the bodies that come to pester her. She is a witness as to how those shafts of light move, can use them to tell the time; and if she counts slowly and rhythmically in her head, she can guess when they will traverse from sofa to floor, and from floor to the pink slippers on her feet.

If on occasion she is certain her slippers ought to be blue it is probably of little consequence, not compared to the movement of light.

Another face appears before her and mouths something she doesn't understand. Grace has given up on words. What good did they ever do anyone, that's what she wants to know. People build things out of words, and the things they build are mostly lies. Lies and empty promises.

There was a man she knew once who said that he didn't give a damn. And she has a vague recollection of another man who said that he would never leave her, no matter what. Were they one and the same? They might well have been. And now they have both abandoned her, even if some young woman keeps telling her that she can get the man who said 'damn' back. Something about him being blown away in the wind — as if a man could be fragile enough to be dismissed quite so easily! The stranger even suggests that he might be trapped in the television, when everyone knows that the only things there are washing powders, dog food, people swimming in crystal clear waters under perfect skies. And there are those charlatans who with their slippery words try to persuade you to be responsible for foreigners, or lame donkeys, or whales.

She smiles to herself. Whales. Some words are easier to hold on to than others, are *worth* holding onto — not that she is going to tell anyone what they are!

Someone says "tea" and she nods because she knows she is supposed to. They seem pleased she has done so; smile when they bring her a cup of something brown which she has no intention of drinking. It seems the least she can do, these small favours. And she wonders if she has always been like that, kind and considerate, putting others' feelings first. It seems likely.

But even as she draws that conclusion she senses something else, something darker; and she looks into the corners of the room expecting to find manifested there the embodiment of what she has lost. The man who said 'damn' perhaps, or the other one. And if it were something else? It cannot be any of the new things she has discovered because they exist in the in-between spaces, in the breathing and sighing of the house, and in the beams of light and the dust dancing in them.

From behind her she hears a sudden roar, and then, right in front of her, that woman again — the one she is sure she has seen before — pushing some noisy contraption across the carpet near the pink slippers that should be blue. And if Grace smiles it is not at the woman, nor the contraption, but because they are making the dust dance in the light even more.

Acknowledgements

- "Where have all the lapwings gone" was first published in *New Contexts: 6*, Coverstory books, 2024
- "Closing his account" was first published in *Verdant Journal*, March 2024

233

www.ingramcontent.com/pod-product-compliance
Lightning Source LLC
Chambersburg PA
CBHW020654120726
47906CB00001B/270